TAMING HER
ITALIAN BOSS

BY

FIONA HARPER

MILLS
BOON®

First published in Great Britain 2014
by Mills & Boon, an imprint of Harlequin (UK) Limited,
Large Print edition 2014
Eton House, 18-24 Paradise Road,
Richmond, Surrey, TW9 1SR

© 2014 Fiona Harper

ISBN: 978-0-263-24112-9

Harlequin (UK) Limited's policy is to use papers that
are natural, renewable and recyclable products and made
from wood grown in sustainable forests. The logging
and manufacturing processes conform to the legal
environmental regulations of the country of origin.

Printed and bound in Great Britain
by CPI Antony Rowe, Chippenham, Wiltshire

*For my readers,
from those who have been with me since
the beginning to those who are picking
one of my books for the first time.
I'm grateful to every one of you.*

CHAPTER ONE

'YOU WANT ME to give you a job?'

The woman staring across the desk at Ruby didn't look convinced. The London traffic rumbled outside the first-floor office as the woman looked her up and down. Her gaze swept down over Ruby's patchwork corduroy jacket, miniskirt with brightly coloured leggings peeking out from underneath, and ended at the canvas shoes that were *almost* the right shade of purple to match the streaks in her short hair.

Ruby nodded. 'Yes.'

'Humph,' the woman said.

Ruby couldn't help noticing her flawlessly cut black suit and equally flawlessly cut hair. She'd bet that the famous Thalia Benson of the Benson Agency hadn't come about her latest style after she'd got fed up with the long stringy bits dangling in her breakfast cereal and convinced her flatmate to take scissors to it.

'And Layla Babbington recommended you try here?'

Ruby nodded again. Layla had been one of her best friends at boarding school. When she'd heard that Ruby was looking for a job—and one that preferably took her out of the country ASAP—she'd suggested the top-class nannying agency. 'Don't let old Benson fool you for a moment,' she'd told Ruby. 'Thalia's a pussycat underneath, and she likes someone with a bit of gumption. The two of you will get along famously.'

Now that she was sitting on the far side of Thalia Benson's desk, under scrutiny as if she were a rogue germ on a high-chair tray, Ruby wasn't so sure.

'Such a pity she had to go and marry that baronet she was working for,' Benson muttered. 'Lost one of my best girls *and* a plum contract.'

She looked up quickly at Ruby, as if she'd realised she'd said that out loud. Ruby looked back at her, expression open and calm. She didn't care what the nanny provider to the rich and famous thought about her clients. She just wanted a job that got her out of London. Fast.

'So…' Ms Benson said in one long drawn-out

syllable while she shuffled a few papers on her desk. 'What qualifications do you have?'

'For nannying?' Ruby asked, resisting the urge to fidget.

Benson didn't answer, but her eyebrows lifted in a what-do-you-think? kind of gesture.

Ruby took a deep breath. 'Well…I've always been very good with kids, and I'm practical and creative and hard-working—'

The other woman cut her off by holding up a hand. She was looking wearier by the second. 'I mean professional qualifications. Diploma in Childcare and Education, BTEC…Montessori training?'

Ruby let the rest of that big breath out. She'd been preparing to keep talking for as long as possible, and she'd only used up a third of her lung capacity before Benson had interrupted her. Not a good start. She took another, smaller breath, giving herself a chance to compose a different reply.

'Not exactly.'

No one had said it was going to be a *great* reply.

Thalia Benson gave her a frosty look. 'Either one has qualifications or one hasn't. It tends to be a black-or-white kind of thing.'

Ruby swallowed. 'I know I haven't got any *tra-*

ditional childcare qualifications, but I was hoping I could enlist with your new travelling nanny service. Short-term placements. What I lack in letters after my name I make up for in organisation, flexibility and common sense.'

Benson's ears pricked up at the mention of common sense. She obviously liked those words. Ruby decided to press home her main advantage. 'And I've travelled all over the world since I was a small child. There aren't many places I haven't been to. I also speak four languages—French, Spanish, Italian and a bit of Malagasy.'

Ms Benson tipped her head slightly. 'You've spent time in Madagascar?' The look of disbelief on her face suggested she thought Ruby had gone a bit too far in padding out her CV.

'My parents and I lived there for three years when I was a child.'

Benson's eyes narrowed. *'Inona voavoa?'* she suddenly said, surprising Ruby.

The reply came back automatically. How was she? *'Tsara be.'*

Benson's eyes widened, and for the first time since Ruby had walked through the office door and sat down she looked interested. She picked up the blank form sitting in front of her and started writing. 'Ruby Long, wasn't it?'

'Lange,' Ruby replied. 'With an *e*.'

Benson looked up. 'Like Patrick Lange?'

Ruby nodded. 'Exactly like that.' She didn't normally like mentioning her connection to the globetrotting TV presenter whose nature documentaries were the jewel in the crown of British television, but she could see more than a glimmer of interest in Thalia Benson's eyes, and she really, *really* wanted to be out of the country when good old Dad got back from The Cook Islands in two days' time. 'He's my father,' she added.

The other woman stopped messing around with the form, put it squarely down on the desk and folded her hands on top of it. 'Well, Ms Lange, I don't usually hire nannies without qualifications, not even for short-term positions, but maybe there's something you could do round the office over the summer. Our intern has just disappeared off to go backpacking.'

Ruby blinked. Once again, someone had heard the name 'Lange' and the real person opposite them had become invisible. Once again, mentioning her father had opened a door only for it to be slammed shut again. When would she ever learn?

'That's very generous, Ms Benson, but I wasn't really looking for a clerical position.'

Thalia nodded, but Ruby knew she hadn't taken her seriously at all. From the smile on the other woman's face, she could tell Thalia was wondering how much cachet it would bring her business if she could wheel Ruby out at the annual garden party to impress her clientele, maybe even get national treasure Patrick Lange to show up.

That wasn't Ruby's style at all. She'd been offered plenty of jobs where she could cash in on her father's status by doing something vastly overpaid for not a lot of effort, and she'd turned every one of them down. All she wanted was for someone to see *her* potential for once, to need her for herself, not just what her family connections could bring. Surely that wasn't too much to ask. Unfortunately, Ruby suspected Ms Thalia Benson wasn't that rare individual. She rose from her side of the desk, opened the office door and indicated Ruby should return to the waiting area. 'Why don't you take a seat outside, and I'll see what I can do?'

Ruby smiled back and nodded, rising from her chair. She'd give Thalia Benson fifteen minutes, and if she hadn't come up with something solid by then, she was out of here. Life was too short to hang around when something wasn't working. Onwards and upwards, that was her motto.

Everything in the waiting area was shades of stone and heather and aubergine. The furniture screamed understated—and overpriced—elegance. The only clue that the Benson Agency had anything to do with children was a pot of crayons and some drawing paper on the low coffee table between two sectional sofas. When Thalia's office door closed, Ruby shrugged then sat down. She'd always loved drawing. She picked up a bright red crayon and started doodling on a blank sheet. Maybe she'd go for fire engine–red streaks in her hair next time they needed touching up....

She spent the next five minutes doing a pretty passable cartoon of Thalia Benson while she waited. In the picture, Thalia dripped sophistication and charm, but she was dressed up like the Child Catcher from the famous movie, locking a scared boy in a cage.

As the minutes ticked by Ruby became more and more sure this was a waste of her time. The only thing she needed to decide before she left was whether to fold the drawing up and discreetly stick it in her pocket, or if she should prop it on the console table against the far wall so it was the first thing prospective clients saw when they walked in the door.

She was holding the paper in her hands, dithering about whether to crease it in half or smooth it out flat, when the door crashed open and a tall and rather determined-looking man strode in. Ruby only noticed the small, dark-haired girl he had in tow when he was halfway to Thalia Benson's office. The child was wailing loudly, her eyes squeezed shut and her mouth wide open, and the only reason she didn't bump into any of the furniture was because she was being propelled along at speed in her father's wake, protected by his bulk.

The receptionist bobbed around him, trying to tell him he needed to make an appointment, but he didn't alter his trajectory in the slightest. Ruby put her cartoon down on the table and watched with interest.

'I need to see the person in charge and I need to see them now,' he told the receptionist, entirely unmoved by her expression of complete horror or her rapid arm gestures.

Ruby bit back a smile. She might just stick around to see how this played out.

'If you'll just give me a second, Mr...er...I'll see whether Ms Benson is available.'

The man finally gave the receptionist about 5 per cent of his attention. He glanced at her, and as he did so the little girl stopped crying for a second and looked in Ruby's direction. She started up again almost immediately, but it was half-hearted this time, more for show than from distress.

'Mr Martin,' he announced, looking down at the receptionist. He stepped forward again. Ruby wasn't sure how it happened—whether he let go of the girl's hand or whether she did that tricksy, slippery-palm thing that all toddlers seemed to know—but suddenly father and child were disconnected.

The receptionist beat Mr Tall and Determined to Thalia's door, knocking on it a mere split second before he reached for the handle, and she just about saved face as she blurted out his name. He marched into the room and slammed the door behind him.

Once he was inside, the little girl sniffed and fell silent. She and Ruby regarded each other for a moment, then Ruby smiled and offered her a bright yellow crayon.

* * *

Max looked at the woman behind the desk. She was staring at him and her mouth was hanging open. Just a little. 'I need one of your travelling nannies as soon as possible.'

The woman—Benson, was it?—closed her jaw silently and with one quick, almost unnoticeable appraising glance she took in his handmade suit and Italian shoes and decided to play nice. Most people did.

'Of course, Mr Martin.' She smiled at him. 'I just need to get a few details from you and then I'll go through my staff list. We should be able to start interviewing soon.' She looked down at a big diary on her desk and started flipping through it. 'How about Thursday?' she asked, looking back up at him.

Max stared back at her. He thought he'd been pretty clear. What part of 'as soon as possible' did she not understand? 'I need someone today.'

'Today?' she croaked. Her gaze flew to the clock on the wall.

Max knew what it said—three-thirty.

The day had started off fairly normally, but then his sister had shown up at his office just before ten and, as things often did when the women in his family were concerned, it had got steadily more chaotic since then.

'Preferably within the next half hour,' he added. 'I have to be at the airport by five.'

'B-but how old is the child? How long do you need someone for? What kind of expertise do you require?'

He ignored her questions and pulled a folded computer printout from his suit pocket. There was no point wasting time on details if she wasn't going to be able to help him. 'I came to you because your website says you provide a speedy and efficient service—travelling nannies for every occasion. I need to know whether that's true.'

She drew herself up ramrod straight in her chair and looked him in the eye. 'Listen, Mr Martin, I don't know what sort of establishment you think I run here, but—'

He held up a hand, cutting her off. He knew he was steamrollering over all the pleasantries, but that couldn't be helped. 'The best nanny agency in London, I'd heard. Which is why I came to you in an emergency. Have you got someone? If not, I won't waste any more of your time.'

She pursed her lips, but her expression softened. He hadn't been flattering her—not really his style—but a few timely truths hadn't hurt his case. 'I can help.' She sighed and Max relaxed just a little. She'd much rather have told him it was impossible, he guessed, but the kind of fee she was measuring him up for with her beady little eyes was hard to say no to. 'At the very least, let me know the sex and age of the charge,' she added.

Max shrugged. 'Girl,' he said. 'Older than one and younger than school age. Other than that I'm not quite sure. Why don't you take a look and see what you think?'

The woman's eyes almost popped out of her head. 'She's here?'

Max nodded. Where the hell else did the woman think she'd be?

'And you left her outside? Alone?'

He frowned. He hadn't thought about that for one second. Which was exactly why he needed to hire someone who would. Anyway, he hadn't left Sofia completely alone. There had been the flappy woman…

Ms Benson sprang from the desk, threw the door open and rushed into the waiting area beyond her office. There, colouring in with the tip of her tongue caught at one side of her mouth, was

Sofia. Max suddenly noticed something: the noise had stopped. That horrible wailing, like an air-raid siren. It had driven him to distraction all day.

'Here…try purple for the flower,' a young woman, kneeling next to Sofia, was saying. Sofia, instead of acting like a child possessed with the spirit of a banshee, just calmly accepted the crayon from the woman and carried on scribbling. After a few moments, both woman and child stopped what they were doing and lifted their heads to look at the two adults towering over them. The identical expression of mild curiosity they both wore was rather disconcerting.

Max turned to the agency owner. 'I want her,' he said, nodding at the kneeling woman who, he was just starting to notice, had odd-coloured bits in her hair.

Benson gave out a nervous laugh. 'I'm afraid she doesn't work here.'

Max raised his eyebrows.

'Not yet,' she added quickly. 'But I'm sure you'd be better off with one of our other nannies who—'

He turned away and looked at the strange pixie-like woman and the little girl again. For the first time in what seemed like weeks, although it had probably only been hours, Sofia was quiet and calm and acting like the normal child he vaguely remembered. 'No. I want *her*.'

Something deep down in his gut told him this woman had what he needed. To be honest, he really didn't care what it was. It was twenty-five to four and he had to get going. 'What do you say?' he asked the her directly.

The woman finished colouring in a pink rose on the sheet of paper she and Sofia were sharing before she answered. She flicked a glance at the agency owner. 'She's right. I don't even work here.'

'I don't care about that,' he told her. 'You have all the skills I want. It's you I need.'

She blinked and looked at him hard, as if she was trying to work out whether he was serious or not. Normally people didn't have to think about that.

'What if the job isn't what *I* need?' she asked. 'I don't think I should accept without hearing the terms.'

Max checked his watch again. 'Fine, fine,' he said wearily. 'Have it your way. We'll interview in the car. But hurry up! We've got a plane to catch.' And then he marched from the offices of the Benson Agency leaving its proprietor standing open-mouthed behind him.

CHAPTER TWO

IT TOOK RUBY all of two seconds to drop the crayon she was holding, scoop up the child next to her and run after him into the bright sunshine of a May afternoon. God did indeed move in mysterious ways!

And so did Mr...whatever his name was.

Those long legs had carried him down the stairs to street level very fast. When she burst from the agency's understated door onto one of the back roads behind Oxford Street, she had to look in both directions before she spotted him heading towards a sleek black car parked on a double yellow.

She was about to run after him when she had a what's-wrong-with-this-picture? moment. Hang on. Why was she holding his child while he waltzed off with barely a backward glance? It was as if, in his rush to conquer the next obstacle, he'd totally forgotten his daughter even existed. She looked down at the little girl, who was quite happy hitched onto her hip, watching a big red double-decker bus rumbling past the end of the road. She might not realise just how insensitive her father was being at the moment, just how much it hurt when one understood how extraneous they were to a parent's life, but one day she'd be old enough to notice. Ruby clamped her lips together and marched towards the car. No child deserved that.

She walked up to him, peeled the child off her hip and handed her over. 'Here,' she said breezily. 'I think you forgot this.'

The look of utter bewilderment on his face would have been funny if she hadn't been so angry. He took the girl from Ruby and held her out at arm's length so her legs dangled above the chewing-gum-splattered pavement. Now it was free of toddler, Ruby put her hand on her hip and raised her eyebrows.

He was saved from answering by the most horrendous howling. It took her a few moments to realise it was the child making the sound. The ear-splitting noise bounced off the tall buildings and echoed round the narrow street.

'Take it back!' he said. 'You're the only one who can make it stop!'

Ruby took her hands off her hips and folded her arms. '*It* has a name, I should think.'

He offered the screaming bundle of arms and legs over, but Ruby stepped back. He patted the little girl's back, trying to soothe her, but it just made her cry all the harder. The look of sheer panic on his face was actually quite endearing, she decided, especially as it went some way to softening that 'ruler of the universe' thing he had going on. He was just as out of his depth as she was, wasn't he?

His eyes pleaded with her. 'Sofia. Her name is Sofia.'

Ruby gave him a sweet smile and unfolded her arms to accept the little girl. She still didn't know whether following this through was a good idea, but the only other option was working for her dad. He'd flipped when he'd found out she'd given in her notice at the vintage fashion shop in Covent Garden.

Considering that her father didn't pay an awful lot of interest the rest of the time, Ruby had been shocked he'd noticed, let alone cared. He was usually always too busy off saving the planet to worry about what his only child got up to, but this had lit his fuse for some reason.

According to him, Ruby needed a job. Ruby needed to grow up. Ruby needed to stop flitting around and settle to something.

He'd laid down a very clear ultimatum before he'd left for the South Pacific—get a proper job by the time he returned, or he'd create a position for her in his production company. Once there, she'd never escape. She'd never get promoted. She'd be doomed to being *What's her name? You know, Patrick Lange's daughter…*for ever.

Sofia grabbed for Ruby as her father handed her back over, clinging to her like the baby lemurs Ruby had got used to seeing in the Madagascan bush. A rush of protective warmth flooded up from her feet and landed in her chest.

She looked up at the man towering above her. 'And, before I get in that car, we might as well continue with the information gathering. I'd offer to shake your hand but, as you can see—' she nodded to Sofia, who'd burrowed her head in the crook of her neck '—it's in use at the moment. I'm Ruby Lange. With an *e*.'

He looked at her blankly, recognising neither her name nor the need for a response. 'And you are?' she prompted.

He blinked and seemed to recover himself. 'Max Martin.'

Ruby shifted Sofia to a more comfortable position on her hip. 'Pleased to meet you, Mr Martin.' She looked inside the dark interior of the limo. 'Now, are we going to start this interview or what?'

Max sat frowning in the back of the limo. He wasn't quite sure what had just happened. One minute he'd been fully in charge of the situation, and the next he'd been ushered into his own car by a woman who looked as if she'd had a fight with a jumble sale—and lost.

She turned to face him, her eyes large and enquiring as she looked at him over the top of Sofia's car seat, which was strapped between them. 'Fire away,' she said, then waited.

He looked back at her.

'I thought this was supposed to be an interview.'

She was right. He had agreed to that, but the truth of the matter was that, unless she declared herself to be a drug-addicted mass murderer, the job was hers. He didn't have time to find anyone else.

He studied his new employee carefully. The

women he interacted with on a daily basis definitely didn't dress like this. It was all colour and jarring patterns. Somehow it made her look very young. And, right there, he had his first question.

'How old are you?'

She blinked but held his gaze. 'Twenty-four.'

Old enough, then. If he'd had to guess, he'd have put her at a couple of years younger. Didn't matter, though. If she could do the job, she could do the job, and the fact that the small bundle of arms and legs strapped into the car seat was finally silent was all the evidence he needed.

He checked his watch. He really didn't have time to chit-chat, so if she wanted to answer questions, he'd dispense with the pleasantries and get on with the pertinent ones. 'How far away do you live?'

For the first time since he'd set eyes on her, she looked surprised.

'Can we get there in under half an hour?'

She frowned. 'Pimlico. So, yes… But why—?'

'Can you pack a bag in under ten minutes?'

She raised her eyebrows.

'In my experience, most women can't,' he said. 'I don't actually understand why, though.' It seemed a simple enough task, after all. 'I believe it may have something to do with shoes.'

'My parents dragged me round the globe—twice—in my formative years,' she replied crisply. 'I can pack a bag in under five if I have to.'

Max smiled. And not just the distant but polite variety he rolled out at business meetings. This was the real deal. The nanny stopped looking quite so confrontational and her eyes widened. Max leaned forward and instructed the driver to head for Pimlico.

He felt a tapping on his shoulder, a neatly trimmed fingernail made its presence known through the fabric of his suit sleeve. He sat back in his seat and found her looking at him. 'I haven't agreed to take the job yet.'

She wasn't one to beat about the bush, was she? But, then again, neither was he.

'Will you?'

She folded her arms. 'I need to ask *you* a few questions first.'

For some reason Max found himself smiling again. It felt odd, he realised. Not stiff or forced, just unfamiliar. As if he'd forgotten how and had suddenly remembered. But he hadn't had a lot to smile about this year, had he?

'Fire away,' he said.

Was that a flicker of a smile he saw behind those eyes? If it was, it was swiftly contradicted by a stubborn lift of her chin. 'Well, Mr Martin, you seem to have skipped over some of the details.'

'Such as?'

'Such as: how long will you be requiring my services?'

Oh, those kinds of details. 'A week, hopefully. Possibly two.'

She made a funny little you-win-some-you-lose-some kind of expression.

A nasty cold feeling shot through him. She wasn't going to back out already, was she? 'Too long?'

She shook her head. 'I'd have been happy for it to be longer, but it'll do.'

They looked at each other for a couple of seconds. Her eyes narrowed slightly as she delivered her next question. 'So why do you need a nanny for your daughter in such a hurry? I think I'd like to know why the previous one left.'

Max sat bolt upright in his seat. 'My daughter? Sofia's not my daughter!'

The nanny—or *almost* nanny, he reminded himself—gave him a wry look. 'See? This is what I'm talking about...*details.*'

Max ignored the comment. He was great with details. But nowadays he paid other people to concentrate on the trivial nit-picky things so he could do the important stuff. It worked—most of the time—because he had assistants and deputies to spring into action whenever he required them to, but when it came to his personal life he had no such army of willing helpers. Probably because he didn't have much of a personal life. It irritated him that this mismatched young woman had highlighted a failing he hadn't realised he had. Still, he could manage details, sketchy or otherwise, if he tried.

'Sofia is my niece.'

'Oh...'

Max usually found the vagaries of the female mind something of a mystery. He was always managing to put his foot in it with the women in his life—when he had time for any—but he found this one unusually easy to read. The expression that accompanied her breathy sigh of realisation clearly said, *Well, that explains a lot.*

'Let's just say that I had not planned to be childminding today.'

She pressed her lips together, as if to stop herself from laughing. 'You mean you were left holding the baby.... Literally.'

He nodded. 'My sister is an...actress.'

At least, she'd been trying to be the last five years.

'Oh! Has she been in anything I've heard of?'

Max let out a sigh. 'Probably not. But she got a call from her agent this morning about an audition for a "smallish part in a biggish film". Something with...' what was the name? '...Jared Fisher in it.'

The nanny's eyes widened. 'Wow! He's really h—' She shut her mouth abruptly and nibbled her top lip with her teeth. 'What I meant to say was, what a fabulous opportunity for her.'

'Apparently so. She got the job, but they wanted her in L.A. right away. The actress who was supposed to be playing the part came down with appendicitis and it was now or never.'

Secretly he wondered if it would have been better if his little sister had sloped despondently into his office later that afternoon, collected her daughter and had gone home. She'd always had a bit of a bohemian lifestyle, and they'd lost touch while she'd travelled the world, working her way from one restaurant to another as she waited for her 'big break'. But then Sofia had come along and she'd settled down in London. He really didn't know if this was a good idea.

Maybe things might have been different if they'd grown up in the same house after their parents had split, but, while he'd benefited from the steadying influence of their English father, Gia had stayed with their mother, a woman who had turned fickle and inconsistent into an art form.

They had grown apart as teenagers, living in different countries, with totally different goals, values and personalities, but he was trying to make up for it now they were more a part of each other's lives.

Gia always accused him of butting his nose in where it wasn't wanted and trying to run her life for her, but she always said it with a smile and she was annoyingly difficult to argue with. Perhaps that was why, when she'd turned up at his office that morning with Sofia and had begged him to help her, her eyes full of hope and longing, he hadn't been able to say no.

'And what about you?' he asked. 'Why do you need a job in such a hurry?'

She rolled her eyes. 'It was either this, or my father was threatening to make me work for him.'

'You don't want to work for the family firm?'

She pulled a face. 'I'd rather jump off the top of The Shard! Wouldn't you?'

Max stiffened. 'I now head up the business my father built from nothing.'

An unexpected stab of pain hit him in his rib-cage, and then came the roll of dark emotion that always followed. Life had been much simpler when he'd been able to bury it all so deep it had been as if it hadn't existed. 'There's something to be said for family loyalty,' he added gruffly. 'For loyalty full stop, actually.'

She looked a little uncomfortable, but waltzed her way out of the awkward moment with a quip. 'Well, I'm quite prepared to be loyal to your family. Just as long as you don't ask me to get entangled with mine. Parents are fine and all that, but I'd rather keep them at a safe distance.'

Max couldn't help but think of his mother, and he decided not to quiz Ruby any further on her motives. It wasn't going to alter whether he hired her or not for a couple of weeks. If this had been for a more permanent fixture in his life, it might have been a different matter.

'So, why do you need a travelling nanny?' Her face lit up. 'Are we going to Hollywood?'

She sounded just like Gia. Max resisted the urge to close his eyes and wish this were all a bad dream, that he'd wake up in bed, his nice, ordered life back.

'I'm taking Sofia to stay with her grandmother,' he said. It was the only possible solution. All he had to do now was convince his mother of that. 'I can't possibly babysit a toddler for the next fortnight, even if I knew how to. I have three weeks to turn around an important work situation and I can't take any time off.'

The shock of realising he'd have to cope with Sofia on his own while Gia was away had been bad enough, but then his biggest client had phoned, slinging a spanner in the works. Now he couldn't afford even an hour off work, let alone a fortnight. He needed time to think. Space. Peace and quiet. And Sofia brought none of those things with her in her tiny, howling package.

Hopefully he'd get Sofia installed at his mother's, then he'd be able to fly back and be at his desk first thing Monday, only half a day lost. It had been Gia's idea, and, while he didn't relish having to take time out to deliver Sofia, at least his sister's moment of destiny had come on a Friday morning. He'd stay overnight to make sure they all settled in and leave the nanny with his mother. He'd thought of everything.

The girl gave him a sideways look. 'So work is important to you? More than family?' She didn't look impressed.

Max gave her one of his patented you-don't-know-what-you're-talking-about looks. *Of course* family was important! That was why he had to seal this deal. He was determined to carry on and finish what he and his father had started together, to ensure that his dad's dream was fulfilled.

'I'm a thirty-something bachelor with a riverside apartment that has split-level floors with no railings, stairs with no banisters and no outside space except a balcony with a hundred-foot drop to the Thames. Do *you* think it would be the responsible thing to allow a child to live there?'

He could see her wrestling with herself, but finally she shook her head.

'Taking her to her grandmother's is the most sensible and practical thing to do—for everybody.'

He looked up. They'd crossed the river now and could only be minutes from her home. If she said no he'd just drop her off and they'd never see each other again. And he'd have to wrestle a screaming Sofia all the way to her grandmother's on his own.

'So, Miss Lange with an *e*, will you take the job?'

She inhaled and held the breath for a few seconds before glancing up at her building, then she let the air out again. 'I have one last question.'

'Which is?'

The corners of her mouth curled up, as if she couldn't quite believe he hadn't mentioned this himself. 'You really are a big-picture kind of guy, aren't you?'

Yes, he was. 'How did you know?'

'There's another detail you've forgotten, a rather important one. If I'm going to be your travelling nanny, I kind of need to know where we'll be travelling to.'

Ah, yes. Another good point. He cleared his throat. 'Italy,' he said. 'We're going to Venice.'

Ruby's hand shot out, her long slender fingers stretched towards him. 'Done.' He half expected her to spit in her palm, but she just looked steadily at him.

He encased her smaller hand in his own, feeling the warmth of her palm, the softness of her skin. Something tiny but powerful tingled all the way up his arm. He shook her hand. 'It's a deal,' he said, his voice rumbling in his own ears. 'You're hired.'

But as he pulled his hand away he started to wonder if he knew exactly what he'd got himself into.

CHAPTER THREE

RUBY SHOULD HAVE realised when the limo driver gingerly put her hastily packed canvas rucksack into the boot that this journey was going to be different. She was used to travelling, used to crowded terminals in international airports teeming with the whole spectrum of human life. She was used to queuing just to buy a bottle of water and browsing the endless shops filled with travel gadgets in order to fill the time. She was used to playing 'hunt the chair' in the departure hall, and dozing on it with her jacket for a pillow when she found one.

She was not used to hushed and elegant lounges in small city airports, free food, drink and entertainment. Even though her father could easily afford to fly business class everywhere, he refused to, preferring what he called 'real' travel. If he wasn't squished into Economy or standing at a three-mile queue at Immigration it wasn't a real trip. Of course, the public loved him for it. Privately, Ruby had always wondered why dust and the ubiquitous Jeep with dodgy suspension were more 'authentic' than air-conditioned coaches these days, but she wasn't daft enough to argue with him. He was disappointed in her enough already.

She sighed. It had been better when Mum had been alive. Even though she'd done exactly the same job, travelled along with him and presented the programmes alongside him, she'd always been good at hugs and sending postcards and presents to boarding school to let Ruby know that just because she was out of sight, it didn't mean she was out of mind. Her father was no good at that stuff. And after she'd died he'd channelled his grief into his work, meaning he lost himself in it more than he ever had done before.

Ruby found herself a spot on the edge of a designer sofa in the lounge and reached for the bowl of macadamia nuts on the table in front of her, only scooping two or three out with her fingers and popping them quickly into her mouth, then she returned to doodling on a paper napkin with a pen she'd pulled out of her bag.

It was supposed to have been easier once the journey got under way. She'd thought that at least the 'travelling' part of being a travelling nanny would be inside her comfort zone. *Wrong again, Ruby.* And she didn't even have anything work-related to do to keep her mind off her awkwardness, because Sofia, obviously exhausted by the sheer graft of tantruming half the day, was stretched out on the plush sofa with her thumb in her mouth, fast asleep and completely unaware of her surroundings.

Her new boss didn't make it any easier. He'd hardly made eye contact with her since they'd left her flat, let alone talked to her. He was a right barrel of laughs.

She filled the short time they had by quickly sketching him as he remained, granite-like and motionless, hunched over his laptop; the only parts of him moving were his eyes and his fingers. She used only a few lines to get the back of his head and his jaw right, leaving the strokes bare and uncompromising, then settled down to reproducing the wrinkles on the arms of his jacket, the soft shock of dark thick hair that was trimmed to perfection at his nape.

Thankfully, once the flight was called and they had to head to the gate and board the plane, Ruby started to feel a little more normal. Jollying a freshly woken toddler along kept her occupied. It wasn't that difficult. Sofia was a sweet child, even if the quiet curiosity hid a will of steel, like her uncle's. Poor child must have been scared and upset when she'd seen her mother disappear out of Max's office without her. It was no wonder she'd screamed the place down.

As the plane began its descent to Marco Polo airport Ruby began to feel the familiar quiver of excitement she always got at arriving somewhere new. She'd always wanted to visit Venice, had even begged her father to go when she'd been younger, but he hadn't been interested. It was a man-made construction, built on stilts in the middle of a lagoon, and the city itself had few open green spaces, let alone rare wildlife—unless you had an unusual passion for pigeons. Ruby didn't care about that. She liked cities. And this one— *La Serenissima*, as it used to be known—was supposed to be the jewel of them all.

It was a disappointment, then, to discover that they weren't going to be arriving in Venice by boat, as many visitors did. Instead Max had ordered a car to take them along the main road towards the city of Mestre, which then turned onto the seemingly endless bridge that stretched from the land to the city across the lagoon.

Sofia began to whine. Although she'd had that brief nap at the airport, the poor little girl looked ready to drop. Ruby did her best to calm her down, and it helped, but what the child really needed was someone she knew. She might have taken to her new nanny, but Ruby was still a stranger. As was her uncle, Ruby guessed. The sooner she was reunited with her grandmother, the better.

The car pulled to a halt and Ruby looked up. Her face fell. Usually, she liked catching the first glimpse of a new place, seeing it as a far-off dot on the horizon, and getting more and more excited as it got closer and closer. This evening, she'd been so busy distracting Sofia back from the verge of another tantrum, she'd missed all of that. They'd arrived at a large square full of buses. They were in Venice at last, and yet this didn't look magical at all. The Piazzala Roma looked very much like any other busy transport hub in any busy city.

People were everywhere. They spilled off the large orange buses that seemed to arrive and leave every few minutes, dragging luggage behind them as they set off on foot, maps in hands; or they queued wearily and waited for the buses to empty so they could clamber inside and head back to the mainland.

The driver started unloading the bags. Ruby took her rucksack from the boot before this one had a chance to be snooty about it, then reached inside and unclipped Sofia from her car seat. The little girl grizzled softly as she clung round Ruby's neck. They walked a short distance to a waiting motor launch on the side of a nearby canal. But Ruby was too busy trying to work out if the sticky substance Sofia had just wiped onto her neck was tears or snot to really pay attention. The boat driver nodded a greeting to Max, and then started up the engine.

For the next few minutes they took a dizzying route through the narrow canals—the equivalent of back streets, she supposed—and she could hardly see more than whitewashed or brick walls, oddly placed ornate windows high up in them, or the odd washing line strung with underwear, waving like unconventional bunting above their heads. But then they emerged onto the Grand Canal and Ruby was glad she was sitting down, with Sofia's weight anchoring her to her seat in the back of the boat, because she surely would have thumped down onto her backside if she'd been standing up.

She'd never seen so many beautiful buildings in one place. All were ornately decorated with arches and windows and balconies. Some were crested with intricate crenellations that reminded her of royal icing fit for a wedding cake. Others were the most beautiful colours, the old stone worn and warmed by both the salt of the lagoon water that lapped at their bases and the soft sun dangling effortlessly in a misty sky.

She was still sitting there with her mouth open when the boat puttered to a stop outside a grand-looking palazzo. Instantly, two uniformed men dashed out of an ornate wooden door and onto the small, private landing stage, complete with the red-and-white-striped poles, and collected their bags and helped them from the boat. One tried to relieve Ruby of Sofia, but the little girl wouldn't have it. She clung so hard to Ruby's neck that Ruby almost choked. She had to make do with letting one of the men steady her as she clambered, a little off balance, onto the small stone jetty.

Ruby looked up. The building was very elegant. Traditional Venetian style, its tall windows topped with almost church-like stonework. Surely nobody real could live anywhere quite so beautiful?

Max must have decided she was dawdling, because he huffed something and turned.

She shook her head slightly. 'Your mother lives *here*?'

He thought she was being slow again. She could tell by the way he was looking at her, a weary sense of disbelief on his features. 'Of course my mother doesn't live here. It's a hotel.'

Maybe it was because she was tired and Sofia felt like a lead weight, or maybe it was because this had probably been the strangest day of her life so far, but she bristled. 'You said we were taking Sofia to see your mother. You didn't say anything about a hotel.'

'Didn't I?'

'No, you didn't,' she said darkly, and then muttered under her breath, '*Details*, Mr Martin.'

He waited until they had walked through the lobby and were whooshing upwards in a shiny mirrored lift before he spoke again. 'This is the Lagoon Palace Hotel. Sofia is tired.' He nodded in her direction, where the child was still clamped onto Ruby's shoulder like an oversized limpet. It was the first time he'd even given a hint he'd remembered his niece existed since she'd taken over. And, consequently, the fact he'd even noticed Sofia was exhausted took Ruby by surprise. 'It'll be a lot less fuss if we settle in here this evening and go and see my mother in the morning.'

Ruby opened her mouth to ask why, then shut it again. A flicker of a look had passed across his features, tensing his jaw and setting his shoulders. She was only too well acquainted with that look. Some people rushed into their parents' arms after a separation, but other people? Well, sometimes they needed a chance to mentally prepare themselves.

She just hadn't expected Max Martin, who seemed to have life buttoned up and marching to his tune, to be one of her fellow throng.

The inside of the Lagoon Palace was a surprise. Ruby had expected it to be full of ornate furniture, antiques and brocade, but the style was a mix of classic and contemporary. The original features of the building were intact, such as the tall marble fireplaces, the plasterwork and painted ceilings, but the decor was modern, with furnishings in bold, bright colours and rich textures.

The suite Max had booked had a main living

area overlooking the Grand Canal and a bedroom on either side. A low, modern sofa in cherry-red velvet faced the windows and two matching armchairs sat at right angles. The end tables were a funky organic shape and the walls were the same colour as the furnishings. Other than that it was all dark wood and pale creamy marble.

Ruby stood in the middle of the living area, mouth open, taking it all in. 'I was expecting something a little more…traditional,' she said to Max as she dropped her rucksack on the floor and let Sofia down from where she'd been carrying her. Sofia instantly thrust her arms upwards, demanding to be picked up again.

Ruby sighed and did as commanded. She needed a moment to get her bearings and having a wailing child wouldn't help. So far she'd felt totally at sea, and she had no idea whether she was looking after Sofia the right way. For all she knew, she could be mentally scarring the child for life.

Her uncle might not have noticed, but she needed to start acting, and thinking, like a real nanny. Tomorrow they'd be meeting Sofia's grandmother, and, if she was anything like her son, she'd be sharp as a tack, and she definitely wouldn't be oblivious to Ruby's shortcomings. The last thing she wanted was to lose this job before it had even started.

'I don't like clutter,' Max said. He took a moment to look around the suite, as if he hadn't really taken it all in before. 'While it's not exactly minimalist, it's as unfussy as this city gets.'

Sofia began to grizzle again, so Ruby carried her across to one of the bedroom doors and looked inside. There was a huge bed, with a sofa with burnt orange velvet cushions at the foot, and large windows draped in the same heavy fabric. Obviously the boss's room. She retreated and checked the door on the opposite side of the living area. It led to a spacious room with twin beds, decorated in brown and cream with colourful abstract prints on the walls. She assumed she'd be sharing with Sofia, at least for tonight.

She was relieved to see each room had its own en suite. It was odd, this nannying lark. Being part of a family, but not really being part of a family. There were obviously boundaries, which helped both family and employee, but Ruby had no idea where to draw those lines. Still, she expected that sharing a bathroom, trying to brush your teeth in the sink at the same time as your pyjama-clad boss, was probably a step too far.

Not that she wanted to see Max Martin in his pyjamas, of course.

For some reason that thought made her cheeks heat, and she distracted herself by lugging Sofia back into the living room, where her new boss was busy muttering to himself as he tried to hook up his laptop at a dark, stylish wooden desk tucked into the corner between his bedroom door and the windows.

'I'm going to put Sofia to bed now,' she told him. 'She ate on the plane, and she's clearly dog-tired.'

Max just grunted from where he had his head under the desk, then backed out and stood up. He looked at Sofia, but didn't move towards them.

'Come on, sweetie,' Ruby cooed. 'Say night-night to Uncle Max.'

Sofia just clung on tighter. Eventually he walked towards them and placed an awkward kiss on the top of the little girl's head. Ruby tried not to notice the smell of his aftershave or the way the air seemed to ripple around her when he came near, and then she quickly scurried away and got Sofia ready for bed.

She put Sofia to bed in one of the twin beds in their room. In the bag her mother had packed for her, Ruby found a number of changes of clothes, the usual toiletries, a few books and a rather over-loved stuffed rabbit.

'Want Mamma,' the little girl sniffed as Ruby helped her into her pyjamas.

Ruby's heart lurched. She knew exactly how that felt, even though her separation from her mother was permanent and at least Sofia would see hers again very soon. But at this age, it must feel like an eternity.

She picked Sofia up and sat her on her lap, held her close, and pulled out a book to read, partly as part of the bedtime ritual, but partly to distract the child from missing her mother. She also gave her the rabbit. Sofia grabbed on to the toy grate-fully and instantly stuck her thumb in her mouth and closed her eyes, giving out one last shudder-ing breath before going limp in Ruby's arms.

Not even enough energy for a bedtime story. Poor little thing.

Ruby put the book on the bedside table and slid Sofia under the covers before turning out the light.

Ruby knew what it felt like to be carted from place to place, often not knowing where you were or who you'd been left with. She was tempted to reach across and smooth a dark curl away from Sofia's forehead, but she kept her hand in her lap.

Usually, she threw herself into each new job with gusto, immersing herself completely in it, but she had a feeling it would be a bad idea for a travelling nanny. This was a two-week job at most. She couldn't get too attached. Mustn't. So she just sat on the edge of the bed watching Sofia's tiny chest rise and fall for what seemed like ages.

When she was sure her charge was soundly asleep, and she wouldn't disturb her by moving, she crept out and closed the bedroom door softly behind her. The living room of the suite was steeped in silence and the large gurgle her stomach produced as she tiptoed towards the sofa seemed to echo up to the high ceilings. It was dark now, and the heavy red curtains were drawn, blocking out any view of the canal. Ruby longed to go and fling them open, but she supposed it wasn't her choice. If her boss wanted to shut himself away from the outside world, from all that beauty and magnificence, then that was his decision.

She could hear her employer through his open bedroom door, in a one-sided conversation, talking in clipped, hushed tones. She glanced over at the desk, where he'd already made himself quite at home. The surface was covered in sheets of paper and printouts, and a laptop was silently displaying a company name that floated round the screen.

Martin & Martin.

Ruby changed direction and wandered over to take a better look. Amongst the printed-out emails and neat handwritten notes there were also half-rolled architectural plans—for something very big and very grand, by the looks of it.

So Max Martin was an architect. She could see how that suited him. He was possibly the most rigid man she'd ever met. Anything he built would probably last for centuries.

She couldn't help peering over the plans to get a better look at the writing on the bottom corner of the sheet.

The National Institute of Fine Art.

Wow. That was one of her favourite places to hang out in London on a rainy afternoon. And she'd seen a display last time she'd visited about plans for a new wing and a way to cover the existing courtyard to provide a central hub for the gallery's three other wings.

Max's voice grew louder and Ruby scuttled away from the desk. She'd just reached the centre of the room when he emerged from his bedroom, mobile phone pressed to his ear. She did a good job of trying not to listen, pretending to flick through a magazine she'd grabbed from the coffee table instead, but, even though she was trying to keep her nose to herself, it was obvious that Max was the front-runner for the institute's new wing, but the clients had reservations.

She finished flipping through the glossy fashion mag and put it back down on the table. To be honest, she wasn't sure what to do now. Did being Sofia's nanny mean she just had to hole herself up in the bedroom with her, never to be seen or heard without child in tow? Or was she allowed to mingle with other members of the family? Seeing as this was her first experience of being a nanny she had absolutely no clue, and seeing as this was Max's first experience of hiring one—even if he had been the kind of person to dole out information without the use of thumbscrews—he probably didn't know, either.

He turned and strode towards her, frowning, listening intently to whoever was on the other end of the phone.

Ruby looked up at him, expecting maybe a nod, or even a blink of recognition as he passed by, but she got none. It was as if he'd totally forgotten she existed. So she became more comfortable studying him. He looked tired, she thought as she watched him pace first in one direction and then another, always marking out straight lines with precise angles. The top button of his shirt was undone and his tie was nowhere to be seen.

It was odd. All day so far, he'd just seemed like a force of nature—albeit in a pristine suit—and now that just the tiniest part of that armour had been discarded she was suddenly confronted by the fact he was a man. And a rather attractive one at that.

His dark hair was short but not severe, and now she knew he had Italian blood in him, she could see it in the set of his eyes and his long, straight nose. The mouth, however, was totally British, tightly drawn in, jaw tense as he grimaced at some unwelcome news and hung up on the caller without saying goodbye. He brought the phone down from his ear and stared at it so hard that Ruby thought it might burst into flames.

That was when he looked up and spotted her sitting where she'd been for the last ten minutes, and it took him by total surprise. She allowed her lips to curve into the barest of smiles and held his gaze. For some reason she liked the fact her presence sometimes ruffled him.

He shoved his phone back in his pocket. 'Is there anything you need?'

His tone wasn't harsh, just practical.

'I was wondering what to do about food.' Her stomach growled again, just to underline the fact. She refused to blush.

He had only just stopped frowning at his phone call, and now his features crumpled back into the same expression, as if he'd forgotten hunger was an option for him, and he was taking time to remember what the sensation was like. Eventually, he indicated a menu on the sideboard. 'Have what you want sent up.'

Ruby nodded. She'd been hoping he'd say that. 'Do you want anything while I'm ordering?'

'No...' His gaze drifted towards the array of papers on the desk and he was drawn magnetically to it. He picked up a sheet and started reading a page of dense text.

Ruby wasn't quite sure if he'd finished saying everything he'd been going to say, but she guessed he'd forgotten he'd actually started talking, so she went and fetched the menu. When she ordered her club sandwich she did it discreetly, so as not to disturb him, and just before she put the phone down she quietly ordered another. He hadn't touched the food on the plane, and she hadn't seen him eat anything all afternoon. He had to get hungry some time, didn't he?

If he did, he showed no sign of it. His eyes stayed on his papers while his fingers rapped out email after email on his laptop. She watched him out of the corner of her eye, slightly fascinated. He was so focused, so intense. He seemed to have an innate sense of confidence in his own ability to do what needed to be done.

To be honest, she was a little jealous.

She'd tried a number of jobs since dropping out of university but none of them had stuck. She wanted what Max had. A purpose. No, a calling. A sense of who she was in this world and what she was supposed to be doing while she was here.

A knock on the door a few minutes later heralded the arrival of her dinner. She opened the door and tipped the room-service guy, then wheeled the little trolley closer to the sofa.

What she needed to do right now was stuff her face with her sandwich, before her stomach climbed up her throat and came to get it. That was the problem, maybe. She could always see the step that was right in front of her, the immediate details—like taking the job this afternoon—but when it came to the 'big picture' of her life it was always fuzzy and a bit out of focus.

She poured a glass of red wine from a bottle she'd ordered to go along with the food and took it, and the other sandwich, over to her boss. He didn't look up, so she cleared a little space at the corner of papers and put the plate down. The wine, however, was more tricky. The last thing she wanted to do was put it where he'd knock it over. Eventually, she just coughed lightly, and he looked up.

'Here,' she said, handing him the glass. 'You looked like you could do with this.'

For a moment he looked as if he was going to argue, but then he looked longingly at the glass of Pinot Noir and took it from her. As he did, just the very tips of their fingers brushed together.

'Thank you,' he said.

Ruby held her breath, then backed away silently. Her face felt hot and she had the sudden urge to babble. She always did that when she was flustered or nervous, and suddenly she was both.

Max, however, didn't notice. It was obvious he was as cool and calm and focused as he'd always been. He put the glass down near the back of the desk and carried on typing the email he'd been working on. Her cheeks flushed, Ruby retreated to the far end of the large sofa and ate her sandwich in silence.

When she'd finished her dinner, she stood up and replaced the empty plate on the trolley, then she hovered for a moment. He hadn't touched either the food or the wine. She wanted to say something, but she didn't know what; then she interrupted herself with a yawn. It was almost ten and it had been a long day. Maybe she should just go and get ready for bed.

Still, as she made her way towards her bedroom door she lingered, fingers on the handle, her eyes drawn to the silent figure hunched over his laptop in the corner. It was a long while before she pressed down on the metal fixture and pushed the door open.

As she got undressed in the semi-dark, careful not to wake the sleeping child, she thought about Max and all his quiet dedication and commitment. Maybe he was rubbing off on her, because suddenly she wanted to rise to the challenge in front of her.

She knew it seemed as if she'd come by this job

almost by accident, but maybe that was just fate sending her a big, flashing neon sign? *This way, Ruby...* Maybe being a nanny was what she was meant to do. Hadn't Max said she was exactly what he needed? And Sofia already seemed very attached to her.

She held her breath as she slid in between the cool cotton sheets and pulled the covers up over her chest. Maybe this was her calling. Who knew? But for the next week—possibly two—she'd have her chance to find out.

Max looked up from his plans and papers and noticed a club sandwich sitting on the edge of the desk. How long had that been there? His stomach growled and he reached for it and devoured it in record time.

Ruby must have put it there. He frowned. Something about that felt wrong.

And not just because taking care of him wasn't part of her job description. He just wasn't used to being taken care of full stop, mainly because he'd carefully structured his life so he was totally self-sufficient. He didn't need anyone to look after him. He didn't need anyone, at all. And that was just as well. While his father had been his rock, he hadn't been the touchy-feely sort, and work had always kept him away from home for long hours. And his mother…

Well, he hadn't had a mother's influence in his life since he'd been a teenager, and even before the divorce things had been…explosive…at home.

A rush of memories rolled over him. He tried to hold them at bay, but there were too many, coming too fast, like a giant wave breaching a sea wall in a storm. That wall had held fast for so many years. He didn't know why it was crumbling now, only that it was. He rubbed his eyes and stood up, paced across the living room of the suite in an effort to escape it.

This was why he hated this city. It was too old, full of too much history. Somehow the past—anyone's past—weighed too heavily here.

He shook his head and reached for the half-drunk bottle of wine on the room-service trolley and went to refill his glass. The Pinot had been perfect, rich and soothing. Just what he'd needed.

He didn't want to revisit any of those memories. Not even the good ones. Yes, his mother had been wonderful when she'd been happy—warm, loving, such fun—but the tail end of his parents' marriage had been anything *but* happy.

Those good times were now superimposed with her loud and expressive fits of rage, the kind only an Italian woman knew how to give, and his father's silent and stoic sternness, as he refused to be baited, to be drawn into the game. Sometimes the one-sided fights had gone on for days.

He took another slug of wine and tried to unclench his shoulder muscles.

His relationship with his mother had never been good, not since the day she'd left the family home in a taxi and a cloud of her own perfume. He hadn't spoken to her in at least a year, and hadn't seen her for more than three.

He looked down at his glass and noticed he'd polished it off without realising. There was still another left in the bottle....

No. He put his glass down on the desk and switched off his laptop. No more for tonight. Because if there was one thing he was certain of, it was that he'd need a clear head to deal with his mother come morning.

CHAPTER FOUR

MAX WALKED OUT of his bedroom then stopped, completely arrested by the sight in front of him. *What the heck?*

And it wasn't the spray of cereal hoops all over the coffee table or the splash of milk threatening to drip off the edge. Nor was it the sight of his niece, sitting cross-legged on the carpet and eating a pastry, no sign of a tantrum in sight. No, it was the fact that the nanny he'd hired yesterday bore no resemblance to the one who was busily trying to erase the evidence of what had obviously been a rather messy breakfast session.

She froze when she heard him walk in, then turned around. Her gaze drifted to the mess in the middle of the room. 'Sofia doesn't like cereal, apparently,' she explained calmly. 'And she felt the need to demonstrate that with considerable gusto.'

He blinked and looked again.

The voice was right. And the attitude. But this

looked like a different girl.... No—woman. This one was definitely a woman.

Gone was the slightly hippy-looking patchwork scarecrow from the day before, to be replaced by someone in a bright red fifties dress covered in big cartoon strawberries. With the full skirt and the little black shoes and the short hair swept from her face, she looked like a psychedelic version of Audrey Hepburn.

Hair! That was it!

He looked again. The purple streaks were still there, just not as apparent in this neater style. Good. For a moment there, he'd thought he'd been having a particularly vivid dream.

'Good morning,' he finally managed to mutter.

She raised her eyebrows.

Max covered up the fact that the sight of all those strawberries had made him momentarily forget her name by launching in with something she'd like—details. 'After breakfast we're going to visit Sofia's grandmother.' He paused and looked at the slightly milk-drenched, pastry-flake-covered child in front of him. 'Would you be able to get her looking presentable by ten?'

The nanny nodded. 'I think so.'

'Good.' Max felt his stomach unclench. 'My

mother is not someone who tolerates an untidy appearance.' And then he turned to go and fire up his laptop, but he could have sworn he heard her mutter, *'What a shocker...'* under her breath.

The water taxi slowed outside a large palazzo with its own landing stage leading up to a heavy front door. They'd travelled for maybe fifteen minutes, leaving the Grand Canal behind and heading into the Castello district of the city.

The building was almost as large at the hotel they'd just left, but where its plaster had been pristine and smooth, this palace was looking a little more tired round the edges. Green slime coated the walls at the waterline, indicating the height of the high tide. Some of the pink plasterwork had peeled off at the bottom of the structure leaving an undulating wave of bare bricks showing.

There were grilles over the ground-floor windows, and the plaster was peeling away there, too, but up above there were the most wonderful stone balcony and window boxes overflowing with ivy and white flowers. The overall effect was like that of a grand old lady who'd had a fabulous time at the ball but had now sat down, a little tired and flustered, to compose herself.

Ruby's eyes were wide as she clung onto Sofia to stop her scrambling ashore before the boat was properly secured.

Max must have read her mind. 'This is Ca' Damiani and, yes, my mother lives here. But she doesn't occupy the whole thing, just the *piano nobile.*'

Ruby nodded, even though she had no idea what that meant.

'A lot of these grand old buildings have been split up into apartments,' he explained as he hopped from the boat and offered to take Sofia from her. 'In buildings like these the floor above ground level was the prime spot, where the grandest rooms of the house were situated—the stage for all the family's dramas.' He sighed. 'And there's nothing my mother likes more than a grand drama.'

His voice was neutral, expressionless even, but she could see the tension in his jaw, the way the air around him seemed heavy and tense. This was not a joyful homecoming, not one bit.

Ruby clambered out of the boat and reached for Sofia's hand, and then the three of them together walked off the dock and up to a double door with a large and tarnished brass knocker. Ruby swallowed as Max lifted it. When it fell the noise rang out like a gunshot, and she jumped. She did her best not to fidget as they waited.

After a short wait the door swung open. Ruby would have expected it to creak, from the age of it, but it was as silent as a rush of air. The woman who was standing there was also something of a surprise. Ruby had expected her to be tall and dark, like Max, but she was petite and her blond hair was artfully swept into a twist at the back of her head. She wore a suit with a dusky pink jacket and skirt and, just like every other Italian woman Ruby had ever met, carried with her an innate sense of confidence in her own style. Not a hair on her head was out of place.

Ruby looked down at her strawberry-patterned skirt. She'd chosen her best vintage dress for today in an attempt to emulate that effortless style, but now she feared she just looked like a sideshow freak instead of *la bella figura*. She held back, hiding herself a little behind Max's much larger frame.

His mother looked at him for a long moment.

No, Ruby thought, she didn't just look. She drank him in.

'Well, you have finally come, Massimo,' she said in Italian, her voice hoarse.

'I've told you I prefer Max,' he replied in English. 'And it was an emergency. Gia needed me. What else could I do? I wasn't going to run out on her, on my family, because things got a little difficult.'

The words hung between them like an accusation. Ruby saw the older woman pale, but then she drew herself taller.

'Oh, I know that it is not on my account that you are here,' she said crisply. 'As for the other matter, I named you, Massimo, so I shall call you what I like.' She glanced down and her face broke into a wide and warm smile. 'Darling child! Come here to your *nonna*!'

Sofia hesitated for a second, then allowed herself to be picked up and held. Ruby guessed that Max's sister must be a more frequent visitor here than he was. After a couple of moments Sofia was smiling and using her chubby fingers to explore the gold chain and pendant around her grandmother's neck. She seemed totally at ease.

When she'd finished fussing over her granddaughter, Max's mother lifted her head and looked at him. 'You'd better come inside.'

She retreated into a large hallway with a diamond-tiled floor and rough brick walls. There were hints of the plaster that had once covered them, and most of the moulded ceilings were intact. However, instead of seeming tumbledown, it just made the palazzo's ground floor seem grand and ancient. There were a few console tables and antiques, and a rather imposing staircase with swirling wrought iron banisters curved upwards to the first floor.

His mother started making her way up the staircase, but when she turned the corner and realised there was an extra body still following them, and it wasn't just someone who'd helped them unload from the boat, she stopped and walked back down to where Ruby was on the floor, ballet-slippered foot hovering above the bottom step, and let Sofia slide from her embrace.

'And who do we have here?' she asked, looking Ruby up and down with interest. Ruby's heart thudded inside her ribcage. Not the sort of girl who usually trailed around after her son, probably. Well, almost definitely.

'This is Sofia's nanny,' Max said, this time joining his mother in her native language. 'I hired her especially for the trip.'

'Ruby Lange,' Ruby said and offered her hand, hoping it wasn't sticky, and then continued in her best Italian, 'It's lovely to meet you.'

Max's mother just turned and stared at her son, tears filling her eyes, and then she set off up the staircase again, this time at speed, her heels clicking against the stone. 'You have insulted me, Massimo! Of all the things you could have done!'

Max hurried up the stairs after his mother. 'I've done nothing of the sort. You're making no sense at all.'

He'd reverted to English. Which was a pity, because when he spoke Italian he sounded like a different man. Oh, the depth and tone of the voice were the same, but it had sounded richer, warmer. As if it belonged to a man capable of the same passion and drama as the woman he was chasing up the stairs.

Ruby turned to Sofia, who was looking up the staircase after her uncle and grandmother. Once again, she'd been forgotten. Ruby wanted to pull her up into her arms and hug her hard. She knew what it was like to always be left behind, to always be the complication that stopped the adults in your life from doing what they wanted. 'What do you say, kiddo? Shall we follow the grown-ups?'

Sofia nodded and they made their way up the stairs. It was slow progress. Sofia had to place both feet on a step before moving to the next one. Her little legs just weren't capable of anything else. When they got halfway, Ruby gave up and held out her arms. The little girl quickly clambered up her and let her nanny do the hard work.

Well, that was what she was here for. Or she would be if Signora Martin didn't think she was so much of an insult that she threw Ruby out on her ear. Max hadn't been wrong when he'd mentioned drama, had he?

When she got to the top of the stairs the decor changed. There was wood panelling on the walls and the ceilings were painted in pastel colours with intricate plasterwork patterns. Every few feet there were wall sconces, dripping with crystals. If this explosion of baroque architecture and cluttered antique furniture was what Max had meant when he'd called Venetian style 'fussy', she could see his point.

The 'discussion' was still raging, in a room just off the landing. The space must have been huge, because their voices echoed the same way they would in a church or a museum. His mother's was emotive and loud, Max's steady and even. Ruby was glad her soft shoes didn't make much noise and she crept in the direction of the raised voices, Sofia resting on her hip.

'You're never going to forgive me, are you?' his mother finally said softly.

Ruby crept a little closer. The room had double doors, which were still standing where they'd been flung open, and she peeked at the interior through the gap next to the hinges.

Max's mother closed her eyes and sadness washed over her features. 'That's why you brought the nanny, wasn't it? You think I'm not fit to look after my granddaughter on my own. Was I really such a terrible mother?'

This was getting too personal, Ruby realised. It was time to back away, leave them to it. She'd just have to find somewhere to hide out with Sofia until the whole thing blew over. Surely there must be a kitchen in this place somewhere?

She retreated a couple of steps, but she'd forgotten that she was much less nimble with Sofia increasing her bulk and she knocked into a side table and made the photo frames and lamp on it jangle.

There was silence in the room beyond. Ruby held her breath. A moment later Max appeared in the doorway and motioned for her to come inside. Ruby would rather have drunk a gallon of lagoon water, but she really didn't have much choice. She hoisted Sofia up into a more comfortable position, tipped her chin up and walked into the room.

It was a grand Venetian salon, with a vast honey-coloured marble fireplace and trompe l'oeil pillars and mouldings painted on the walls in matching tones, with mythic scenes on the walls in between. A row of arched windows leading onto a stone balcony dominated the opposite side of the room, and three large green sofas were arranged in a C-shape, facing them. But the sight that Ruby was most interested in was the stiff figure in the pink suit standing in the middle of the room.

'Ruby isn't here to usurp you, Mamma. I hired her partly to help me bring Sofia over here with minimum fuss, but also because I thought she could help you. Why should you have to cancel your social engagements, alter your plans, for the next couple of weeks because of Gia's work problems?'

The other woman's features softened a little, and she looked a little ashamed. She turned to face Ruby and held out her hand. Ruby let Sofia down and the little girl ran to the window to look at a speedboat that had just shot down the medium-sized canal beyond.

'Serafina Martin.' She smiled warmly and shook Ruby's hand firmly but very briefly. 'But everybody calls me Fina. I apologise most sincerely for not welcoming you to Ca' Damiani when you first arrived, but I do so now.'

Ruby replied in her best Italian. 'Thank you, Signora Martin, for your welcome and for opening your home to me, if you do decide you could do with my help. I'm afraid this is my first job as a nanny so I've been thrown in at the deep end.' She glanced at Max, who was watching her carefully. 'You'll probably have to help me more than I'll help you.'

A small flicker of approval, and maybe relief, passed across the other woman's features. Fina tilted her head. 'Your Italian is very good.'

Ruby kept her smile demure. 'Thank you.'

Fina's gaze swept over her dress and then up to her head. 'But your hair is not. Purple?'

She shrugged. 'I like it.'

For the longest moment Fina didn't move, didn't say anything. She didn't even blink, but then she smiled. It started in her eyes and moved to just lift the corners of her mouth. '*Bene.* What do I know?

I am old and out of touch, probably, and I like a woman who follows her own path.' And then she turned and swept out of the room. 'Come, Massimo! We have to decide what you are going to do about this child.'

Max stared at his mother. 'What do you mean you want me to stay here, too?'

That hadn't been the plan at all. The reason he'd brought Sofia here was because now was definitely not the moment to take an impromptu holiday. He couldn't let everything he and his father had worked for slide.

His mother did that infuriating little wave of her hand, suggesting he was making a mountain out of a molehill. 'You made a very good point,' she said airily. 'I do have plans this week, including earning a living. I can't take time off at this short notice.'

Max's jaw dropped. 'You have a *job*?'

She turned her head to look at him. 'Why is that so hard to believe? Yes, I have a job. I work for a real estate company in the mornings, helping them dress and present their luxury properties.'

He shook his head, hardly able to believe it.

'You are straying from the point, Massimo. It

is not important where I work, but how we are going to do the best for Sofia.'

He frowned. 'I know that, Mamma. That's why I came to you in the first place. It just isn't possible to keep her in London with me. There's a work issue that's at a very crucial point and I can't give her the time and attention she deserves.'

'You know I adore having Sofia with me, but do you think I keep this place running because money falls from the sky? I also have urgent work to do.'

He shot a glance across at his travelling nanny. She was kneeling on the carpet, helping Sofia build a house out of colourful blocks. Max didn't know where they'd come from. His mother must have had them stashed away somewhere. 'But that's why I brought Ruby.' He'd thought of everything, made it simple and easy. Why was his mother turning this into a problem when there was none?

'The poor child is upset and away from her mother. When I'm not here, she needs to be with someone she knows.'

She looked the picture of innocence, perched on the edge of a green damask sofa. The high windows let in the soft light of the May morning, basking her in an almost saintly glow.

'But she doesn't know me, either.'

His mother frowned. 'I thought Gia had said that you were in regular contact now.'

'We text, mainly,' he mumbled. 'And she comes into the city to have lunch every couple of months, but she doesn't usually bring Sofia with her.'

He rather suspected she deliberately chose the days Sofia was at nursery, so she could come up to town and have a few hours to herself. She very kindly always picked the best places, and always let her brother pay.

'Texting is not communicating! It is not the same as a smile or a hug or a warm word. One cannot build relationships through one's phone.'

He shrugged and his mother did another one of her famous hand gestures. Not the little elegant hand-flap, this one. Both arms flew above her head and she stood up and walked over to stare out of the windows onto the canal below. 'Then this is the perfect opportunity for you to get to know her. You really should. She is your only niece, after all.'

If that wasn't an example of his mother's own brand of circular logic, he didn't know what was.

'But she cries every time I look at her,' he said, more than a little exasperated. 'I try to talk nicely to her but it doesn't seem to make any difference. I'd stay if it were different, but it's hardly the best thing for Sofia to leave her with me on my own if that's the case.'

'But you won't be on your own,' his mother said, far too silkily for his liking. 'You'll have Ruby.'

They both transferred their gazes to the travelling nanny. Ruby, who must have sensed two pairs of eyes on her, stopped what she was doing and looked up at them from under her fringe. Max had a lightning stab of revelation. Ruby had already proved very useful when it had come to Sofia, perhaps she could be more useful still. Perhaps he could enlist her as an ally. He sent her a silent message with his eyes.

Ruby's lips twitched. 'It's true,' she said, looking at his mother. 'She does cry most of the time when she's near him. They don't know each other at all. He's not even sure how old she is.'

His mother reached across and slapped his leg. Quite hard, actually. 'Massimo! Honestly!'

She turned to look at Ruby, and Max had the feeling he was being pointedly ignored for the moment. 'She'll be three in a month,' his mother said in Italian, and then she and Ruby had a brief exchange about when Sofia's birthday was and what sort of things she liked to do. He was quite surprised at how good the nanny's Italian was, to be honest. He hadn't even known she spoke it. Just went to show his instincts about her had been right, even if she did make each day look as if she'd raided a different fancy dress shop.

However, when Ruby and his mother started getting into what time was bedtime and favourite snacks, he decided that enough was enough. He stood up and walked closer to them. 'Can we just get back to the matter in hand?' he said, maybe a little abruptly.

Both women stopped talking and looked at him. They wore identical expressions. Max had the horrible sinking feeling that maybe he'd been right about Ruby being a good ally. He just wasn't sure she was his.

'I need to know this kind of stuff, actually,' she told him. 'And you weren't much help.'

Details.

He could almost hear Ruby's mental whisper that followed.

That was enough to set his mother throwing her hands in the air again. When she'd calmed herself down by walking over to the fireplace and back again, she fixed him with a determined expression. Max knew that look. It meant she'd made up her mind about something, and budging her from that viewpoint was going to be about as easy as asking the whole of Venice to pick up her skirts and move a little further out into the lagoon.

'I have made a decision,' she announced. 'I would like nothing more than to have my lovely granddaughter here for a visit.'

He let out a breath he hadn't been aware he'd been holding. 'Thank you, Mamma.'

His mother drew herself up and put on her most regal air. 'But I will allow it on one condition.'

What?

'I won't take Sofia unless you stay, too,' his mother told him, folding her arms across her chest. 'You cannot live your life cloistered away in that stuffy office of yours, communicating to those you love through bits of technology. It's high time you lived up to your family responsibilities, Massimo.'

Max almost choked. *His* family responsibilities? That was rich!

He opened his mouth to argue, but didn't get very far. He became aware of a small but insistent tugging on the left leg of his trousers and looked down to find his niece standing there. She was trying to pull him in the direction of the pile of blocks on the rug near the fireplace.

His mother just smiled at him. 'She's not crying now, my darling son, and you said you'd stay if she stopped.' She looked over at her granddaughter. Warmth and joy flared in her eyes. 'It seems I am not the only one who has made my mind up about this—Sofia has, too.'

CHAPTER FIVE

MAX AND HIS MOTHER had had a long conversation out on the balcony, ironing out the details of her ultimatum. When they returned, Fina knelt down on the carpet beside Ruby and Sofia and joined in their game of piling up bricks into tall towers for Sofia to knock down again.

Fina smiled and laughed, totally absorbed in her granddaughter, while her son stood, towering and silent on the fringes of the room. Ruby shot him a sideways look and found him staring back at her. She swallowed. She felt a little guilty that she'd ended up unwittingly providing Fina with leverage to use against him, but not guilty enough to regret she'd done it.

Despite Fina's superior manner and haughty words, Ruby had seen the way she'd looked at Max. That was a mother hungry for her son's company and, just like a child who'd settle for negative attention when they couldn't get praise, in desperation she'd taken whatever she could get.

Funnily, Ruby warmed to Fina for that. She wished her own father looked at her that way sometimes, but she'd never once got the impression from him that he was hungry for more of her company. No, he'd seemed perfectly content to push her out of the nest at an early age.

'I'd better go and check out of the hotel and get our bags,' Max finally growled.

Ruby stood up and brushed her skirt down. 'I'll help you.' That was the least she could do.

He scowled at her, indicating she'd done enough already. She ignored it and followed him as he headed out of the door. She had to trot to keep up with him as he marched down the corridor and down the sweeping staircase.

'So, what's going on?' she finally asked. 'I presume we're staying, for a short while, at least.'

Max sighed. 'My mother and I have come to an…arrangement.' He shuddered slightly, as if the idea of compromise was an abhorrent concept.

He was doing it again: failing to fill her in on the important stuff. 'Which is?'

Max stopped on the stairs and turned, hands still in pockets. 'My mother has agreed she will care for Sofia when she's free, with your help, of course, but only if I stay for a minimum of seven days. Otherwise she's happy to escort us all to the airport where we can catch the next plane back to London.'

Ruby's face crumpled into a bemused smile. 'She'd really do that?'

He grunted and set off again. 'You have no idea how stubborn my mother can be when she puts her mind to it.'

Ruby didn't reply to that. The only response that came to mind was that maybe he was more like his mother than he realised, and she'd got herself into enough trouble already with him this morning.

She studied the back of his head carefully as she followed him down the stairs. Did he really not get that this ultimatum had nothing to do with his sister's childcare issues and everything to do with Fina wanting to repair the gaping breach in her family? Ruby had also gone to extreme lengths to get just a crumb of her father's attention in her teenage years, and she understood completely why Fina had done it.

'And what about the Institute of Fine Art? The plans?'

He turned as he reached the ground floor, looking surprised.

'Couldn't help overhearing you on the phone last night. And then there are the drawings littered all over the suite…'

Max ran a hand through his hair as they emerged from the palazzo onto the dock and wearily took in the grand and crumbling buildings around them. 'I'm in Venice…' he said, and she sensed he was quoting his mother verbatim. 'The most beautiful city in the world. What better inspiration could I have?'

Thankfully, Max discovered his mother hadn't disposed of the little motor launch that had once been his grandfather's. By the looks of it, she'd kept it in immaculate condition. The varnish wasn't peeling and the navy paint on the sides was fresh and thick. He jumped in, stood behind the small windscreen and slid the key into the ignition to start it up. Ruby, unmissable in that damn strawberry dress, clambered in hesitantly then plopped down on the seat at the back. He put the boat in gear and set off through some of the narrower canals.

He'd spent every summer here as a boy, even before his parents' divorce, and it amazed him that, even though he hadn't driven a boat here in more than two decades, the old routes and back-doubles came to him easily. His passenger didn't say much. She spent most of the journey to the Lagoon Palace looking up at the tall buildings, her mouth slightly open, eyes wide. It was only when they moored the boat a short distance from the hotel's private jetty, where only the dedicated shuttles from the bus and train stations were allowed to dock, that Ruby began to talk again.

'So, what are the finer points of your agreement with your mother? You can't have spent that long arguing about it without going into details.'

He sighed as he led her up a narrow cobbled *calle* between buildings and out onto a wider one that led to the foot entrance of the hotel. He'd known he wouldn't be able to win his mother over to his plan from the moment he'd stepped out onto the balcony with her. He had, however, managed to broker a deal that meant his stay here would be on his terms.

'I have conceded to spend a couple of hours each morning with Sofia while my mother is at work and to attend a family dinner each evening.' He couldn't help the slight tone of disgust in his voice at the word 'family'.

She kept up pace, slightly behind him. 'And what did she concede?'

'That I should have the rest of the time to work on my design and do my business.'

'Will that do?'

He stared straight ahead and looked grim. 'It will have to.' As they entered the hotel through the street entrance he sighed. 'What's the alternative? At least this way I'm only tied up for seven days, instead of two weeks or more in a totally unsuitable apartment. Aside from the fact you'd be trying to stop Sofia breaking her neck every moment of the day, I've only got one bedroom.'

Ruby swallowed and her face grew just a little closer to the shade of her dress. 'No, I can see that would be a...' she swallowed again '...problem.'

'I don't know why she does these things. For some reason my mother isn't happy unless she's creating havoc in everyone else's lives as well as her own.' He shook his head.

They'd arrived at the suite now, and the next quarter of an hour was spent packing up their belongings. And then they checked out and headed back to the boat. Max carried his bag, his laptop case and his document tube, and she took care of her own rucksack and Sofia's bag.

He decided to take a less direct, but maybe more scenic, route back. If she'd liked the little crumbling buildings of the back canals, she'd love some of the palazzos on the Grand Canal. He pointed a few of them out to her, telling her a few of the famous stories connected with them, many of which he guessed had been embellished over time with a healthy drop of the Venetian love for drama and spectacle. She chatted back, asking him questions and laughing at the more ridiculous tales, so it kind of took him by surprise when she suddenly said, 'I don't think she's done this to cause trouble, you know. I think she just wants to spend time with you and, yes, she's gone about it a back to front kind of way, but she's not asking anything terrible, is she?'

He didn't say anything. Just stared straight ahead. Suddenly he didn't feel like playing tour guide any more.

He should have remembered this one was different, that she wasn't like his employees at the firm, that she liked to say things she shouldn't and be inquisitive. None of them had ever dared to comment on his personal life. But then he'd never given any of them a personal tour of Venice, either.

He thought about what she'd said and let out a low growl of a laugh.

'What?' she asked, never one to miss an opportunity to stick her nose in.

'Now, maybe, my mother seems like that,' he said gruffly, 'but she's a hypocrite.'

Despite the bustle and noise of the city—the purr of outboard motors, the noise of the seagulls and pigeons and the ever steady hum of a million tourists' exclamations—the air around them went very still. He'd shocked her into silence, had he? Well, good.

'She deserted my father and left him broken-hearted. He never got over it. So don't talk to me about family loyalty.'

He turned to look over his shoulder, wanting some grim satisfaction in seeing her squirm, but instead he found her looking at him, her eyes large and warm. He looked away again.

'How old were you when she left?' she asked softly, almost whispering.

He forgot to ask how she'd guessed, too caught up in a sideswipe of memories that left him gripping the steering wheel so hard it burnt his fingers. 'Fourteen,' he answered hoarsely. 'She said she didn't want to disrupt my education, so she took Gia and left me in London.'

There was a hint of uncertainty in her voice this time. 'That was thoughtful, wasn't it?'

He made that same almost animalistic sound that could pass as a laugh again. 'It was an excuse. I'm too like my father, you see. Or I was. He died five months ago.'

There was a shuffling noise behind him. He couldn't resist a quick glance. Now he'd got what he'd wanted. Her cheeks were flushed red and she was looking down at her flat little black ballet pumps.

'Don't get sucked in,' he warned her. 'She's not what she seems. Nothing is what it seems in this city.'

Nothing is what it seems in this city.

Ruby heard the words inside her head as she stood outside the library door.

It was pure Venice, wasn't it? To have a proper room designated as a library in your palazzo, not just a flat-pack bookcase stuffed under the eaves in your poky little attic flat. Max had decided to use it as his office while he was here, and he was inside now. She could hear him tapping away on his laptop keyboard, along with the odd rustle of paper.

Not even you, Max Martin, she thought, as she knocked softly on the door. Or should that be *Massimo*?

All she got in response was a grunt. She took it as an invitation.

Max didn't look up straight away when she pushed the door open and slid inside to stand with her back pressed against the wall, hands tucked behind her. The library was small compared to some of the other rooms in the apartment, but it shared the same high ceilings and leaded windows. Two of the four walls were filled with bookshelves, and Max sat at a desk placed up against the dark green silky wallpaper of one of the other walls.

It had been a whole twenty-four hours since she'd seen him doing exactly the same thing in the hotel suite, but somehow she felt as if she were looking at a completely different man.

She'd thought him a robot, a machine, but she'd seen the bleakness in his eyes when he'd talked about his family that morning. There was a lot more inside there than met the eye. Maybe even a man with true Italian blood coursing through his veins, a man capable of revenge and passion and utter, utter devotion. The fact that the wounds of his childhood still cut deep, that he could neither forgive nor forget, showed he was capable of more than this grey, concrete existence. But like some of the crumbling buildings of this city, all that emotion was all carefully hidden behind a perfectly built façade.

He pressed the enter key with a sense of finality and turned to face her.

'I've just put Sofia to bed, and I wondered if you'd like to go and say goodnight? She's asking for you.'

His chair scraped and he moved to get up. Ruby pushed away from the wall and clasped her hands in front of her. She cleared her throat. 'I have something to say before you go.'

He stopped moving and looked at her.

She inhaled and let it out again. 'I'd like to apologise for what I said earlier. I didn't mean to butt in.'

She'd expected his face to remain expressionless, but she saw a subtle shift in his features, a softening. 'Thank you.'

He made to go forward and her mouth started off again before she could ask herself if it was a good idea or not. 'I know what it's like, you know.

My relationship with my father has always been difficult. But I pretend I don't care, that it doesn't get to me. That it shouldn't matter after all these years…but it does.'

She was rambling, she knew she was. But she couldn't seem to shut up.

'So I just wanted to say that I won't comment on your family any more and that I'll try and be a little bit more professional in the future.'

He'd been right. She should keep her nose out. Not in the least because this silent, dedicated man was starting to tug at her heartstrings, but also because she was just the nanny, and getting sucked in definitely wasn't part of her job description.

He nodded and glanced towards the door. 'I'd better go and see Sofia before she falls asleep.' And then he walked down the wide corridor without looking back.

Ruby sagged back against the library wall and looked up. She hadn't noticed before, but painted cherubs were dancing on the ceiling, blowing flutes and twanging harps. For some reason, she got the feeling they were mocking her.

If there was one room Max hated more than any other in his mother's house, it was the dining room. Most people were left speechless when they walked inside for the first time, at least for a few moments, then the exclaiming would begin.

Apparently, his great-grandfather had had a fondness for whimsy, and had commissioned an artist to paint the whole room so it resembled a ruined castle in a shady forest glade. Creepers and vines twined round the doorway and round the fireplace. Low down there were painted stone blocks, making the tumbledown walls, and above, tree trunks and leaves, giving glimpses of rolling fields beyond. It even carried on up onto the ceiling, where larks peered down and a pale sun shone directly above the dining table. It was all just one big lie.

The table only filled a fraction of the vast space, even though it seated twelve. Max sat down at one of the three places laid at one end and scowled as his mother sat at the head and Ruby sat opposite him. He hadn't liked being manoeuvred into this whole arrangement and he wasn't going to pretend he liked it any more than he was going to pretend they were sitting in a real forest glade enjoying the dappled sunshine. He was just going to eat and get out of here. The plans he'd left on the desk only a few minutes ago were already calling to him.

'My family were successful merchants here in Venice for five hundred years,' his mother told Ruby as they tucked into their main course. 'But now I live more simply and rent the other parts of the house out.'

Max saw Ruby's eyes widen at the word 'simply'. As always, his mother had no grip on reality, and no awareness of how other people carried on their lives. He tuned the conversation out. His mother was busy regaling Ruby with stories from the annals of their family history, both triumphant and tragic. He'd heard them a thousand times, anyway, and with each telling the details drifted further and further from the truth.

Then his mother ran out of steam and turned her attention to their guest. Well, not guest…employee. But it was hard to think of Ruby that way as she listened to his mother with rapt attention, eyes bright, laughter ready.

'So, tell me, Ruby, why did you decide to become a nanny?'

Ruby shot a look in his direction before answering. 'Your son offered me a job and I took it.'

Fina absorbed that information for a moment. 'You didn't want to be a nanny before that?'

Ruby shook her head.

'Then what were you?'

Max sat up a little straighter. He hadn't thought to ask her that during their 'interview'. Maybe he should have. And maybe Ruby was annoyingly right about *details* being important on occasion.

Ruby smiled back at his mother. 'Oh, I've been lots of things since I left university.'

He leaned forward and put his fork down. 'What course did you take?'

'Media Studies.'

Max frowned. 'But you don't want to work in that field, despite having the qualification?'

She pulled a face. 'I didn't graduate. It was my father's idea to go.' She shook her head. 'But it really wasn't me.'

His mother shot her a sympathetic look. 'Not everyone works out the right path first time.'

Max snorted. If these dinners had been his mother's plan to soften him up, it was backfiring on her. Every other word she uttered just reminded him of how she'd selfishly betrayed the whole family. She might not have been a Martin by birth, but she'd married into the institution, and if there was one rule the family lived by it was this: loyalty above all else.

If his mother had heard the snort, she ignored

it. 'You must have had some interesting jobs,' she said to Ruby, smiling.

Ruby smiled back. 'Oh, I have, and it's been great. I've made jewellery and I worked in a vineyard.'

'In France?' Fina asked.

Ruby shook her head. 'No, in Australia. I did that the year after I left university. And then I just sort of travelled and worked my way back home again. I tended bar in Singapore, worked on a kibbutz in Israel. I did a stint in a PR firm, I joined an avant-garde performance company—that was too wacky, even for me—and I've also busked to earn a crust.'

His mother's eyebrows were practically in her hairline. 'You play an instrument?' she asked, taking the only salvageable thing from that list.

Ruby gave her a hopeful smile. 'I can manage a harmonica and a bit of tap dancing.'

Lord, help them all! And this was who he'd thought was exactly what he needed? No wonder his sensible plan was falling to pieces.

'And will you stay being a nanny after this? Or is it on to the next thing?' he asked.

She shook her head. 'I don't know. I know this

sounds stupid, but I see the way my father loves his work, and I want to find something that makes me feel like that.'

His mother leaned forward. 'What does your father do?'

Ruby froze, as if she realised she'd said something she shouldn't. She looked up at them. 'Oh, he makes nature programmes.'

'What? Like Patrick Lange?' his mother exclaimed, clapping her hands. 'I loved his series on lemurs! It was fascinating.'

'Something like that,' Ruby mumbled.

Now it was Max's turn to freeze. *Lange?*

'Your father's Patrick Lange?' he asked, hardly able to keep the surprise from his voice. The man seemed such a steady kind of guy. Max could hardly believe he had a daughter like Ruby.

She nodded and returned to eating her pasta.

'How marvellous,' his mother gushed and then the smile disappeared from her face. 'Oh, I'm so sorry about your mother, Ruby. It was such a tragedy. She was such a wonderful woman.'

Ruby kept her head down and nodded.

Max racked his brains. There had been a news story... Oh, maybe fifteen years ago? That was it. Martha and Patrick Lange had always presented their nature documentaries together until she'd contracted some tropical disease in a remote location while filming. She'd reassured everyone she was fine, that it was just a touch of flu, and had carried on, reluctant to abandon the trip. By the time they'd realised what it was, and that she'd needed urgent treatment, it had been too late. She'd died in an African hospital a week later.

Max watched Ruby push her pasta around her plate. He knew what it was like to lose a parent, and it had been bad enough in his early thirties. Ruby could have only been…what? Nine or ten?

'Anyway,' Ruby suddenly said, lifting her head and smiling brightly. 'I'd like to find my perfect fit. My niche.'

His mother, who had finished her meal, put her knife and fork on her plate and nodded. 'There's no sense in doing something if your heart isn't in it.'

There she went again. He'd just about forgotten about being angry with her for a moment, distracted by Ruby's sad story, but she had to dig herself another hole, didn't she? It just proved she would never change.

His mother must have noticed the expression on his face, because she stopped smiling at Ruby and sent him a pleading look. He carried on eating his pasta. She tried to smile, even though her eyes glistened in the light from the chandelier.

'Well, maybe being a nanny will be your niche. You're a natural with Sofia.'

'Thank you, Fina.' Ruby smiled, properly this time, and the gloom of her previous expression was chased away. How did she do that? How did she just let it all float away like that, find the joy in life again?

'Massimo wanted to be an architect since he'd got his first set of building blocks,' his mother said. Her face was clear of the hurt he'd seen a few moments ago, but he could hear the strain in her voice. 'He always wanted to follow in his father's footsteps.' She turned to him. 'He would have been so proud to know you'd secured the commission for the Institute of Fine—'

Max's chair shot back as he stood to his feet. 'Don't you dare presume to speak for my father,' he said through clenched teeth. His insides were on fire, yet his skin felt as cold as ice. 'In fact, I'd rather you didn't mention him at all in my presence.'

And then he turned and strode from the room.

CHAPTER SIX

MAX STARED AT SOFIA, who was currently sitting on one of his mother's sofas, staring at him expectantly. Gone was the sunshine of the previous day, replaced by a low, drizzly fog. It would probably clear up by the afternoon, but that didn't help him now.

There would be no walk this morning, no playing ball games in the street or a nearby square. Unsurprisingly, there weren't many parks in Venice, so children had to make do with whatever outside space the city presented to them. He tried to rack his brains and think what he'd done as a boy on his visits here, but most of his memories were of when he was older, involving boats or other children.

Ruby walked into the room. He hadn't seen her since last night, and had almost got used to the bright strawberry-covered dress. Her attire was once again completely different, but somehow it seemed less of a jump this morning. Today she looked like a groupie from a rock band, with skinny jeans, a black T-shirt and a multitude of necklaces and bangles. Her dark, purple-streaked hair also seemed to be standing up a little more than usual.

'Good morning,' she said.

Max nodded.

Ruby must have seen the panic in his eyes, because she smiled that soft little I'm-trying-not-to-make-it-look-as-if-I'm-laughing-at-you smile. He gave up any pretence of competence.

'What do I do?' he asked, gesturing towards the windows.

She shrugged. 'Do something she likes to do.'

Marvellous suggestion. Great. That was the whole point. 'But I don't *know* what she likes to do.'

He searched around the room. His mother didn't have many toys, just a few in the bottom section of an antique sideboard. He opened the door and started to rummage. When he was halfway through pulling things out, most of them puzzles and board games far too old for his niece, he felt a light touch on his shoulder. He twisted his head and found Sofia grinning at him. 'Dat!' she announced firmly, pointing to a cardboard box.

Max reached for it and opened the lid. It contained the brightly coloured wooden blocks that Sofia had been playing with yesterday. As he stared at them, the way they were worn, how the paint had been knocked off some of the corners and edges, he realised they'd once been his. Sofia nodded, walked over to the large rug that filled the middle of the room and sat down on it, waiting.

Well, at least he knew what to do with bricks, even if they were this small. He started arranging them into a small structure, but Sofia wasn't happy with that. 'Build pinsess!' she said firmly, tugging at his shirtsleeve.

Max looked at her. 'Huh?'

'Build pinsess,' she repeated, looking at him as if he should have no trouble obeying her command. He looked up at Ruby helplessly.

'I think she's saying "build princess".'

He was still lost.

Ruby chuckled. 'I think she wants you to build her a fairy-tale castle.'

Max looked down at his rather square, half-finished house. Great. Now the Institute of Fine Art weren't the only ones who weren't pleased with an original Martin design.

'What does a fairy-princess castle look like?'

Ruby got down on the rug beside them and started gathering bricks. 'The basics are there,' she said. 'You just need to embellish a little.'

She leaned forward to pick up another brick and Max caught the scent of her perfume. He would have expected her to wear something bold and eye-watering, like too-sweet vanilla or pungent berries, but it was a subtle mix of flowers and spices. It made him forget where he'd been about to place the next brick.

He shook himself and found somewhere, even though he was sure he'd had a different spot in mind when he'd picked the thing up.

They finished the main structure then added turrets and a drawbridge. Ruby even went and found a blue scarf from her luggage and they circled it round the castle like a moat. Sofia took a role as site manager, instructing the adults where she wanted the next tower built and letting them know in no uncertain terms when their efforts didn't meet her expectations.

'She's reminding me of someone else I know,' Ruby muttered under her breath.

Max hid a smile. Seriously, he was not that bad. She reached for a red triangular brick at the same time he did and their hands bumped. She pulled back and rested her bottom on her heels. 'No, you have it. You're the expert.'

He picked it up and dropped it into her hand. 'This isn't a job I can accomplish on my own. I think the finishing touches require some definite feminine input to come up to our patron's high standard.'

She grinned back at him. 'She is a bit of a slave driver.' And then she put the brick above the main gate, making a porch, instead of the obvious place where he would have put it on top of the central turret. When she'd finished she stood up and brushed the carpet fibres off her black jeans.

'Where are you going?' he asked, realising he was disappointed she was leaving.

He told himself it was because he needed her there as backup, that he didn't want to be left alone with Sofia. What if she started crying again?

'It's lunch time,' she said, smiling. 'I think Sofia is getting hungry.'

Max checked his watch. So it was. He'd forgotten how much he'd loved these blocks as a boy, how many rainy days just like this one he'd spent in this room, building forts and skyscrapers and alien space stations.

He stood up and surveyed the creation they'd made together. Despite its flouncy, OTT design, he was quite proud of himself. And Ruby and Sofia, obviously. This really was a spectacular castle. He'd enjoyed himself, remembered just how much joy could be had from building and creating when the pressure wasn't on. And he'd enjoyed the good-natured banter and arguments about which door should go where and just how ridiculously high Sleeping Beauty's tower should be. Instead of feeling burdened and irritated, he felt…

It took him a while to name the sensation. Probably because it had been absent from his life for so long.

He felt relaxed.

'That's you relieved of duty for the morning, then,' Ruby said and held out her hand for Sofia and asked her if she'd like lunch in Italian. Sofia nodded vigorously and began to tell Ruby exactly what she'd consent to eat. The list consisted of mainly chocolate and flavours of ice cream. Ruby just smiled and led her away and Max was left staring at Sofia's castle.

The smile slowly slid from his face. The tiny rainbow-coloured castle might have turned out well, but he still had no idea how to add the same flair to his design for the institute. He stuffed his hands in his pockets and trudged back to the library. For some reason, he didn't think turrets and a moat would be a hit with his clients.

Rather than the pearly mist of the day before, which had draped the whole city in soft, off-white tones, the next morning was bright and loud and colourful. Instead of setting the blocks up in the living room, Max led Ruby and Sofia outside to the dock.

A minute later they were zipping through canals heading for somewhere Max said was a prime spot for what he had in mind. Ruby stared at the 'equipment' he'd brought with them that sat in the bottom of the boat. She guessed they must be doing fishing of some kind, because there were a couple of buckets, some nets and a line of dark wire, wrapped round a plastic reel, with a weight and a hook at one end.

She looked down at the toddler in her arms. Didn't fishing require patience and silence? She wasn't sure how much of a good idea this was.

She didn't have the heart to mention that to Max, though. All traces of the frown that had been permanently etched into his forehead since she'd first met him had disappeared, and he looked calmer, more relaxed, as he drove the little boat through narrow and wide canals, manoeuvring it expertly with only a slight twist of the wheel here and there.

They moored alongside a wide path beside a smallish canal. They were deep in the heart of the city, far enough off the beaten track to have left most of the tourists behind. Max hopped out of the boat and held out his hands for the tackle. Ruby passed him Sofia first, and reminded him to hold her hand tightly. She then picked the buckets and nets up and placed them on the edge of the stone path before clambering out herself.

'What now?' she asked, slightly breathlessly.

Max stared at the opaque green water. 'Now we put our line down and see if we can catch any crabs.'

'Crabs?' That wasn't what she'd been expecting at all.

He nodded. 'Every Venetian child knows how to fish for crabs. At certain times of year, when young ones have shells that are still soft, they are considered a local delicacy.'

'Are you sure Sofia's going to—?'

'I don't know,' he said frankly. 'But why don't we give it a try?'

There wasn't much Ruby could say to that, so she stood by and lent a helping hand where she could, holding on to Sofia while Max carefully explained to her what they were going to be doing and started to put some bait on the hook. He didn't let Sofia touch that bit of the line, but lowered it slowly into the dark water, allowing her to hold on to the plastic reel, but keeping his hands over hers.

They waited for a short while and then he slowly drew the line up again. Nothing. Ruby waited for Sofia to start fidgeting, but she seemed to be fascinated. She clumsily helped Max unreel the line again, frowning in concentration.

Ruby almost laughed looking at the pair of them. She didn't know why she hadn't seen it before, but the family similarity smacked her right between the eyes. The same dark eyes, same cheekbones. They even pursed their lips in the same manner as they stared at the dark twine hanging in the water.

After a minute or so, Max helped Sofia wind the line up again, and this time a tiny green-and-brown mottled crab was hanging from the end. It was hanging on with grim determination, as if it had decided it was *his* dinner on that hook and he wasn't giving it up for anybody.

Sofia squealed. Ruby shot forward, meaning to comfort her, but she realised when she saw the little girl's eyes shining that the noise had been one of delight, not fear. In fact, Sofia was so pleased with her catch that she reached out to grab it as Max tried to gently shake it from the line into a bucket he'd filled with canal water.

Then came another squeal. This one high-pitched and urgent. It seemed Sofia had been a little too enthusiastic, and the crab had thought her a little too tempting, because it had clutched on to her with its free pincer. Ruby quickly darted in and shook it away, but Sofia's eyes filled with tears and she looked at her hand in horror. 'Naughty!' she said vehemently. 'Bad fish!'

Ruby scooped her up and gave her a hug, then bent to kiss the red patch on her finger. The skin wasn't broken and she was probably more surprised and offended than in real pain. She pulled back and smiled at the little girl. 'He just liked you so much he didn't want to let go,' she told her.

Sofia's eyes grew wide. 'Fish *like* me?'

Ruby nodded. 'He's a crab, not a fish, and, yes, I think he thought you looked very tasty.'

Sofia screwed up her face and chuckled heartily. 'Silly fish,' she said leaning over the bucket and peering at her catch. 'No bite Sofia. Kiss.' And she puckered up her lips and bent over farther. Ruby caught her quickly before she got any other ideas.

'Why don't we see if we can find him a friend?' And she indicated where Max was waiting with the crabbing line.

Sofia grinned. 'Want lots and lots friends.'

So that was what they did for the next forty-five minutes—found lots and lots of friends for the little green-and-brown crab. Ruby and Max worked as a team, keeping a firm hold on Sofia when she got over-excited and tried to lean too far over the water, and dealt with crabs and bait when needed. After the first handful of attempts they settled into an easy rhythm, giving them lulls in the action while the bait dangled in the water.

Ruby took an opportunity to look around at the buildings. She wished she had her sketchpad with her—and a free hand—so she could draw them. 'There are so many wonderful shapes to be seen in this city,' she said, sighing. 'What's that called?' She showed Max the building on the far side of the canal, where the stonework around a window curved to a point at the top.

'It's an inflected arch,' he said.

'It makes me think of far-off lands and tales of Arabian nights.'

'It's interesting that you say that, because a lot of Venetian architecture has Eastern influences. Merchants travelled to the Byzantine Empire and traded with the Moors and they came back and combined those shapes with the European gothic architecture to create a unique style.'

She pointed to another building. 'And what about those ones? They're beautiful. At first it just looks like intricate shapes, but then you can see that the fussier patterns are actually made up of intersecting circles.'

He turned to look at her and didn't say anything for a few moments. 'You have a good eye for shapes.'

She shrugged and then bent down to help Sofia shake another crab off her line into the bucket. 'Thank you. I like to draw sometimes. I suppose it's just something I've picked up.'

Max took the line from his niece for a moment and worked out a few tangles before giving it back to her. 'Is that what you've been doing when

I've seen you scribbling away in that notebook of yours?'

She nodded. She hadn't realised he'd noticed. 'It's just a hobby. Nothing impressive, really.'

'You haven't thought of making a career out of it?' He gave her a dry smile. 'Seeing as you've tried everything else?'

'Ha, ha. Very funny. Go for the easy target, why not?' Everyone else did.

'Seriously, if you love it so much, why don't you do something with it?'

She tipped her head to one side. 'You mean, like you did?'

'I suppose so.'

She looked down at the water below them, at the way the light bounced off the surface, moving constantly. 'I don't think I'd be able to do what you do. It's very structured and disciplined. When I draw, I just go with the flow. I see something that interests me and I capture it. I'm not sure you can make a career out of that.'

'You have plenty of discipline,' he said. 'Look at the way you are with Sofia. And sometimes you need that creative spark to liven all that structure up.' He let out a long sigh and stared at the buildings across the water.

'More fish! More fish!' Sofia shouted, jumping up and down so hard she almost toppled into the canal. Ruby kept a firm hand on her as she shook the most recent catch into the bucket to join his friends. Sofia did it so vigorously that Ruby was sure the poor thing must have a concussion.

When Sofia was happily dangling the line in the canal again, Ruby looked at Max. 'What's up?' she asked. 'Was it something I said?'

He sighed again and crouched down to look at where Sofia was pointing at some silvery fish swimming near the surface of the water. 'No. It's something I said.'

She waited for him to stand again.

'It's a commission for the Institute of Fine Art,' he told her. 'I've worked for months on a preliminary design that I'm really proud of, but the board say they're not sure about it.'

Ruby shook her head. She couldn't believe that. The designs she'd glimpsed were amazing. They were totally Max, of course. No frills. No fuss. Nothing ostentatious. But there was an elegance to the simplicity. A pared-back beauty. 'Why on earth not?'

He shrugged. 'I think the actual phrase they used is that they want more "wow factor".'

A screech from around knee level interrupted their conversation. Ruby hadn't noticed it while she'd been talking to Max, but the bucket was now almost full and the crabs were scrambling over each other in an attempt to climb out.

Max knelt down next to his niece. 'It's time to put them back now,' he said matter of factly and tipped the bucket over to let a stream of crustaceans, legs flailing, fall back into the salty lagoon water.

'No!' The exclamation was loud and impassioned and followed immediately by a stream of hot tears. 'Want friend! Want friend!'

Ruby grabbed for the bucket and righted it. Only three crabs remained in the bottom.

Sofia stopped shouting and sniffed. 'Want take fish home.'

Ruby crouched down beside her, put an arm round her shoulders and joined her in looking into the bucket. She might be wrong, but she thought one of the three crabs left might be the little one they'd caught first. 'We can't take them back to Grandma's, sweetie. They belong here in the water. It's their home. We just picked them out to say hello for a little bit.'

Sofia let out a juddering sigh.

'Why don't we put the last ones back one by one and say a nice goodbye to them?'

Sofia frowned. 'Come back 'morrow say hello?'

Ruby smiled. 'If you want.'

The little girl nodded. Ruby looked inside the bucket and then up at Max. 'How do we...?'

Quick as anything his hand plunged into the bucket and he pulled out a crab. 'There's a trick to it. If you hold them at the back of the shell like this, they can't reach to pinch you.'

He held the crab up for Sofia to see. She puckered up her lips. 'Kiss fish?' she asked.

Ruby's heart just about melted.

'Not too close,' she said softly, imagining what Fina would say if her precious granddaughter came home with pincer holes in her lips. 'Just blow a kiss.'

Sofia blinked then puffed heartily on the crab, who was so shocked it stopped waving its legs around angrily and went still. A deep rumble started in Max's chest then worked its way up out of his mouth in the most infectious of chuckles. Ruby looked up at him, eyes laughing.

'That's a first,' he said, smiling, and then he gently plopped the crab back into the canal.

They followed the same routine with the next

crab, too, but when they came to the last one, Ruby asked, 'Can I pick it up?'

Max nodded. He put the bucket down on the cobbles and took hold of Sofia while Ruby took off her watch and stuffed it in her jeans pocket. She inhaled, then dipped her hand into the cold water and aimed her forefinger and thumb for the parts of the shell the way she'd seen Max do it. It wriggled away a couple of times, but then she gripped more firmly and lifted the crab out of the water.

'I did it!' she exclaimed. 'For a moment there I didn't think I was— *Ow*!'

A searing pain shot through her finger, making her eyes water. She blinked the moisture away, slightly breathless, to find an angry little crab attached to her hand. She was sure it was scowling at her.

'Ow, ow, ow...' she yelped and started shaking her hand backwards and forwards. Anything to make it let go!

Eventually the force of the swinging must have got the crab, either that or it lost its grip on her wet hands, because it shot off, landed on the paving stones a couple of feet away then scuttled to the edge and flung itself into the canal.

'Ow,' Ruby said again, just to make her point, even though her attacker probably neither heard nor cared.

She looked down as her finger started to throb. That had definitely *not* been the original crab with the delicate little pincers that hadn't punctured Sofia's finger. This one had been mean and angry, and blood was now seeping from a hole in her skin.

'Here, let me look,' Max said and swiftly caught up her hand.

Ruby would have expected his examination to be practical and thorough, and it was, but she hadn't expected it to be so gentle. She looked at him, head bowed over her hand as he ran his fingers over the area surrounding her war wound, and for some reason the sight of his dark lashes against his cheek made her feel a little breathless.

Sofia hugged her left leg. 'No cry, Ruby. Fish no want let go.'

Despite the thudding of her pulse in her index finger, Ruby couldn't help but smile. She looked up to find Max doing the same, but his face was very close. She blinked and sucked in a breath.

'Kiss better!' Sofia commanded.

Ruby would have been okay if she hadn't

realised he was holding his breath, too, that he seemed to be stuck looking at her the same way she was looking at him.

'Go on, Uncle Max! Kiss better.'

Slowly Max raised her hand, not taking his eyes off her until the moment he bent his head and softly pressed his lips to where Ruby's finger was throbbing. The sensation spread out from that finger, through the rest of her body, until she couldn't breathe, couldn't move. Max seemed to be similarly affected, because even though he'd lowered her hand again he still held it between his warm fingers.

Sofia tugged Ruby's trouser leg, seeking a response she hadn't yet got. 'Him no want let go.'

Ruby swallowed. 'I know, sweetheart.' And as she spoke the words she slid her hand out of Max's and looked away to where the crab had plopped into the water.

'I think it'll be fine,' he mumbled, then busied himself collecting up the fishing equipment and putting it back in the boat.

CHAPTER SEVEN

MAX SPENT THE REST of the afternoon in the library with the door shut. He tinkered with his plans for the institute until his eyes were gritty and his brain was spinning. It didn't help that every time he wasn't 100 per cent immersed in what he was doing he kept having strange flash-backs.

He kept seeing Ruby's slightly swollen and bleeding finger. Inevitably that led to memories of looking up into her eyes. He hadn't noticed their colour before. Warm hazel. Not green. Not brown. But a unique pairing of the two that was slightly hypnotic. He hadn't been able to look away, hadn't been able to let go. And then he'd gone and kissed her finger. What had all that been about?

Okay, he knew *exactly* what that had been about. He might not have been in the mood to date since his father's death, finding himself drawn to his own company, filling his hours with work, but he was no stranger to desire.

He stopped tweaking a design for a staircase he had up on his computer screen and deleted all the last fifteen changes he'd made. It had been better before. Now it was *more* boring, if that was even possible. He'd seen a hundred different staircases like it in a hundred different buildings.

He pushed back from the desk, stood up, began to pace.

He needed something different. Something unique.

Like those eyes...

No. Not like those eyes. They had nothing to do with it.

For heaven's sake! It wasn't even as if Ruby was anything like the kind of women he usually went out with, the kind he'd hardly noticed he'd stopped seeing: cultured, sophisticated, beautiful.

He sighed. And next to Ruby they seemed like clones churned out by a production line.

In comparison, she was strangely easy to be with. There was no game-playing. No second-guessing whether he'd accidentally said the wrong thing because he was being subjected to some secret test. If Ruby thought he'd overstepped the mark, she just told him in no uncertain terms.

There was a knock at the door and he stopped

pacing and faced it, grunted his permission to enter. A moment later his travelling nanny popped her head round the door. 'Your mother wanted me to let you know that dinner is served.'

She looked down and away, as if she was feeling awkward. When she looked up again, a faint blush stained her cheeks.

The air grew instantly thick. Max nodded. 'Thank you,' he managed to say. 'I'll be along in a minute.'

She smiled hesitantly and shut the door again.

Max ran a hand through his hair and swore softly. Was he imagining it, or had she got prettier since that afternoon?

He went over and sat back down at his desk. He clicked over to his email and read a few messages to distract himself, although what they contained he couldn't have said. When he felt a little more his usual self, he rose and went to the dining room, lecturing himself en route.

You have no business noticing her eyes, warm hazel or otherwise. She's your employee. Get a grip and get over it.

Thankfully, he was sitting opposite his mother this evening at dinner, and Ruby was off to one side, so he didn't catch her gaze while they ate their…whatever it was they ate. He kept his concentration on his plate as his mother once again pounced on their guest as both willing audience and source of conversation.

'Maybe being a nanny will be your niche after all,' she told Ruby. 'You're a natural with Sofia, and she's already very fond of you.'

Ruby smiled at her. 'Thank you. I'm loving spending time with her, too, and spending time in Venice. This really is the most remarkable place.'

Fina's chest puffed up with pride in her home. 'You've never visited before?' she said.

'No. I always wanted to, though.'

Fina clapped her hands. 'Well, then we must make sure we don't work you too hard, so you get time to see some of the sights! But the best time of day to see the city is the hour leading up to sunset, don't you think, Massimo?'

Max let out a weary sigh. 'I suppose so.'

Ruby smiled and sipped her glass of water. She'd refused wine, seeing as she was still on duty. 'I'm sure it is, but I may have to wait until my next visit for that. By the time I've got Sofia bathed and in bed, it's nearly always dark.'

Fina rose from the table to go and fetch the dessert from the sideboard. 'Then Massimo must take you before he goes back to London. Don't worry about Sofia. I'm sure her *nonna* can manage bedtime alone for one night.'

They both turned to look at him.

He should say no. Make an excuse that he had too much work to do, or tell his mother to drive the boat herself, but he looked back at Ruby, her eyes large and expectant, and found himself saying, 'Okay, but later in the week. And as long as we're not out too long. I have work to do.' And then he returned to attacking his vegetables.

The women went back to chatting again but a while later Ruby piped up, 'Oh! I almost forgot. Before Sofia went to bed, she insisted I give this to you.' She pushed a piece of paper in his direction. 'I was going to let her do it herself, but you seemed to be so busy, so I just…didn't.' She shrugged. 'Well, here it is, anyway.'

He reached out and pulled the scrap towards him, careful not to brush her fingers. From the thick, riotous turquoise crayon that graced the sheet of paper, he could tell the colouring was Sofia's, but the drawing, that was all Ruby's. He smiled as he looked at it.

She'd drawn one of the crabs they'd caught that afternoon in dark ink. The little crab hanging on the end of the fishing line looked full of person-ality, feisty and ready to take on the world if any-one dared try to catch him and tame him. It really was rather good.

'I think you caught him perfectly,' he said, and made the mistake of looking up at her. 'You've got that devilish expression down pat.'

She didn't say anything. Just smiled. And her eyes warmed further.

Max returned his attention to his plate.

He forced himself to remember the conversation that had taken place round this dinner table only a few evenings ago. It didn't matter how nice her eyes were, or how relaxed he felt around her, it would be foolishness in the highest degree to be bewitched by that.

Ruby Lange was a drifter. She'd said so her-self. She didn't finish what she started, always tempted to run after something better and brighter and shinier.

He didn't need a woman like that in his life. He'd seen what his mother had done to his father, hadn't he?

He returned his gaze to his plate.

Pork. They were eating pork.

He'd do well to keep his mind on concrete things

like that. On his work. On his commission, his final gift to the parent who'd stuck around to raise him.

No more distractions, no matter how tempting.

The following evening Ruby approached dinner with a plan. Max was going home in just under forty-eight hours and still he was treating his mother like the enemy.

However, he'd softened up with Sofia nicely. He no longer held her as if she were an unexploded bomb, and interacted quite easily with her now. Sofia, who maybe had been lacking a positive male role model in her life, simply adored him. It was clear a bond was forming between them.

Surely the potential was there with Fina, too? All he needed was to be thrown in the deep end a bit, as he had been with Sofia.

So Ruby deliberately decided not to natter on at dinner time this evening, hoping it would encourage mother and son to converse. But as they waded their way through the main course, the only sound in the cavernous dining room was the clinking of cutlery and the dull thud of glasses being picked up and set down again.

Fina kept looking at him, willing him to glance

her way, but mostly, unless he was reaching for the salt or refilling his glass, Max refused. As the meal wore on Ruby could sense more and more nervous energy in the woman sitting beside her. Fina must sense her chance for reconciliation ticking away with the hours and seconds until Max's flight back to London. It didn't seem as if he'd be in a hurry to return any time soon, either.

Eventually, Fina cracked. She put down her knife and fork and stared at him for a few seconds before opening her mouth. 'Massimo. You've been having such a wonderful time here with Sofia these last few days.'

Max glanced up so briefly Ruby doubted he'd even had time to focus on Fina. He grunted then turned his attention to his plate.

Fina shot a nervous look at Ruby and Ruby nodded her encouragement.

'Ruby's been telling me all about your crabbing expeditions.'

Another grunt. This time without eye contact.

Fina swallowed. 'I was thinking that maybe I'd invite the whole family to visit for the festival of San Martino in November. You used to love decorated biscuits of Martino on his horse, remember?' She laughed. 'You once asked me if we were cousins of the saint, because our last names were so similar.'

Max carried on cutting his chicken, and only when he'd precisely severed a chunk, put it in his mouth and chewed and swallowed it thoroughly, did he answer his mother. 'I don't think I'm going to be able to spare the time from work. If this commission goes through it'll be full steam ahead until the new year.' And then he went back to dissecting his meal.

Fina nodded, even though her son wasn't watching, and hung her head over her plate.

Ruby glared at him. She wanted to fish that little crab they'd met the other day out of the canal and attach it to his nose! He was being so stubborn.

Didn't he know what a gift this was? Maybe Fina hadn't been the perfect mother, but she was trying to make up for it now. Surely that had to mean something? And there had to be good reasons why a woman as warm and caring as Fina had walked away from her marriage. She might try and act blasé, but Ruby couldn't believe she'd done it on a whim, whatever Max might think.

Fina rose from her seat. 'I promised Renata upstairs that I would look in on her. She's not been feeling very well,' she said, and walked stiffly from the room.

Max pushed his plate away. Ruby glared at him. 'Couldn't you just even give her a chance?'

He lifted his head and looked at her. His eyes were empty, blank like the statues topping so many of the palazzos nearby. 'It's not your business, Ruby. What happens in my family is my concern.'

She stared back at him, words flying round her head. But she released none of them, knowing he was speaking the truth and hating him for it. So much for the bond she'd thought they'd forged over the last few days.

She rose and followed Fina out of the room. 'Thank you,' she said as she reached the doorway, 'for putting me firmly in my place.'

At least an hour passed before Max emerged from the library. The apartment was totally quiet. Sofia must be fast asleep and he hadn't heard his mother return from visiting her neighbour.

Everything was dark—well, almost. A few of the wall sconces were lit at the far end of the corridor near the salon. His footsteps seemed loud as he walked down it and entered the large room. In here it was dark, too, with just one lamp turned on near the sofas, making the cavernous space seem smaller and more intimate. He looked for Ruby's dark head against the cushions, for a hint of a purple streak, but there was no one there.

He was about to turn and leave the room, but then he heard a shuffling noise and noticed the doors to the balcony were open. He could just make out her petite form, leaning on the stone ledge, staring out across the water. Taking in a deep breath, he walked over to the open door and stood in the threshold.

'I can hear voices,' she said, her tone bland, 'and I think it must be someone close by, but there are no windows open upstairs and no boats going by.'

'It's just another quirk of this city,' he said. 'Sounds seem oddly hushed at some times and magnified at others. Even a whisper can travel round corners.'

She nodded. Whoever had been talking had stopped now and silence grew around them.

What a pity it wasn't silent inside Max's head. He could hear another whispering voice now, one telling him to apologise. It wasn't the first time he'd heard that voice, but he usually managed to outrun it when it prompted him to do anything as dangerous as letting down his guard, admitting he was wrong, but Venice was amplifying this sound, too, making it impossible to ignore.

Or maybe it was Ruby who did that to him.

Sometimes she looked at him and he felt as if all the things he'd held together for so long were slowly being unlaced.

He should go, retreat back to the library, to the safety of his plans and emails. That was where he'd built the fortress of his life, after all—in his work. Just like his father before him.

Ruby didn't ask anything of him. Didn't demand as his mother would have done. Instead she kept staring out into the night, a faint breeze lifting her feathery fringe.

Max stepped forward. 'I was rude earlier on,' he said. 'I'm sorry.'

She kept her elbows resting on the stone balustrade and turned just her head, studied him. 'I accept your apology, but you spoke the truth.'

She was right, he realised. That was something they always did with each other, whether they wanted to or not. 'Even if it was, I shouldn't have said it the way I did.'

Ruby's cheeks softened and her smile grew. 'Thank you.' She straightened and looked back inside. 'Sofia's appetite for things to colour in is insatiable. I was going to get some outlines done to give me a head start in the morning, but I couldn't resist slipping out here for a moment.'

She moved to go back inside, and his arm shot out across the doorway, blocking her. He didn't know why he'd done that. He should have let her go. Ruby tipped her head and frowned at him, her delicate features full of puzzlement, her eyes asking a question. A question he didn't know the answer to.

But other words found his lips, words he hadn't even realised were his. 'I find it hard to be here… This is the first time I've seen her since my father died.'

She looked back at him, understanding brimming in her eyes.

'She broke him, you know, when she left. Everyone always said he was the same old Geoffrey, hard as steel, never letting anything get to him, but they didn't know him the way I did.'

She moved a little closer, placed a hand on the arm that wasn't blocking her exit, the one that was braced against the rough stone of the balustrade. 'You're angry with her,' she said in a low voice. It wasn't a question.

He nodded. He'd been angry with her for years. It had started as a raging fire that only the indignation and passion of a teenage boy knew how to fan, and had solidified into something darker and deeper. 'Since the day of his funeral I haven't been able to ignore it any longer. I want to but I can't.'

He broke away from her and walked a few steps down the balcony, away from the doors. Ruby, of course, followed him. He heard the soft pad of her ballet pumps on the stone. 'You have to know that it's illogical, that his death wasn't her fault. They've been separated for years.'

He twisted to face her abruptly, his face contorting. 'But that's just it. It *is* her fault. You should have heard some of the things she used to scream at him.' He shook his head. 'And he never once lost his temper. It was the effort of living with her, then living without her, that brought on his high blood pressure.'

Ruby stepped closer. 'Is that how he died?'

He nodded. 'He had a stroke—a little one at first, but while he was in the hospital a bigger one struck, finishing him off.'

He felt the rage boiling inside him now. It was all so perilously close to the surface that he was scared he would punch straight through the five-hundred-year-old wall into the salon.

'She's hurting, too,' Ruby said.

He forced himself to focus on her. For a moment the red haze behind his eyes had blurred his vision.

'Can't you forgive her?'

He shook his head, unable to articulate his answer. No, he didn't think he could. He didn't even know if he'd be able to contain it again, let alone quench it.

She must have seen the tension in his expression, because she stepped even closer, this time so he could smell that maddening elusive perfume. 'You've got to let it go, Max. You can't bury it all inside.' Her eyes pleaded with him. 'If you do it might damage you the same way it damaged him.'

He knew she was right. He just didn't know if he knew how. Or even wanted to.

There was the tiniest noise in the back of his head, something snapping. But instead of releasing his anger he'd unleashed something else. It was also something he couldn't keep buried any longer, and it had nothing at all to do with his mother and everything to do with the firecracker of a woman standing in front of him.

Slowly he leaned forward, and watched Ruby's eyes widen. Darken. He slid his hand behind her neck, relishing the feel of her bare skin, the soft wisps of her hair, until he cupped her head and drew her to him. And then he unleashed the full force of all he was too weary to hold back any longer in one scorching kiss.

Ruby knew she should have frozen, knew she should have slipped out of his arms and retained some degree of decorum. Unfortunately, she wasn't that sensible. Instead of reminding him of the barrier between them, the one that no proper nanny would cross, she let him sledgehammer through it as he ran hot kisses down the side of her neck.

She'd never been one for holding back and she certainly didn't do so now. She ran her hands up his chest, grabbed his shirt collar and lifted herself closer, abandoning herself to the feel of his skin upon hers, his body pressed so tight against her own she felt breathless.

He slid his hands down the curve of her back to her waist, emphasising her femininity against his hard, straight masculinity. He kissed her again and she felt them both teeter on the edge of something, threatening to topple headlong into goodness knew what.

Oh, sweet heaven. She'd been right. When Max Martin let loose there was sizzle and passion and consuming fire, and all of that force was concentrated on her now, at the point where his lips were urgently seeking hers again. It was glorious.

It was also very stupid.

Max must have had an identical revelation at the same time, because he froze, his hands circling her waist, and then he stepped back, effectively dropping her back from her tiptoes onto her flat feet. She swayed, the sudden lack of solid, Max-shaped support and the cold air rushing between their bodies putting her off balance.

'I'm so sorry,' he almost stuttered, a look of complete horror on his face. 'That was totally inappropriate.'

Ruby's lips were still throbbing and her hormones still singing the 'Hallelujah Chorus'. She blinked and stared back at him. *Inappropriate?* That was not a word a girl wanted to hear after the hottest kiss of her life.

He shook his head and strode past her and back into the salon. She watched him go, a gnawing feeling growing in her stomach. She couldn't let him leave like this. This wasn't his fault. She had to let him know that she'd been just as much a part of it as he had been. She heaved in a much-needed lungful of night air and ran after him. 'Max!'

He turned as he passed through the double doors into the corridor.

'You don't have to… I mean, it wasn't just…' She trailed off, unable to find the words. He looked so thoroughly wretched. Part of her sank, but another part wanted to reach out to him, to soothe that crumpled expression from his face.

She'd pushed him too far, when he'd been feeling too raw, and he'd lost control. She got that. But maybe it was a good thing. Maybe loosening up in one area of his life would have a knock-on effect?

But it wasn't just that. The way he'd kissed her, hard and hungry, verging on desperate. He had to feel it, too, this weird attraction, crush…whatever. She wasn't alone in this.

She opened her mouth to speak, hardly knowing how to form the question, but at that moment Fina appeared at the top of the stairs and spotted them farther down the corridor. The atmosphere had been thick around her and Max anyway, but now it became so dense it turned brittle.

Fina walked up to them and looked at her son.

Any hint of the distress she'd shown earlier was gone, replaced by a brisk and prickly demeanour. 'It's your last night tomorrow, Massimo.'

With what looked like supreme effort, Max dragged his gaze from Ruby and turned it to Fina. 'I know that,' he replied.

Ruby looked between mother and son. In an earlier century, an atmosphere like this would have been dispersed by cocking pistols and marching twenty paces in opposite directions. She hoped that Fina would say something conciliatory, forgiving her son his outburst instead of nursing her own pain into hardness.

Tell him you love him, Ruby wanted to yell. *Tell him he's everything in the world to you.* Max might not see it, but she did. It was evident in every breath Fina took.

But Fina stared back at her son. It seemed she'd learned a thing or two from her buttoned-up husband about staying granite-like in the face of pain. She nodded. 'Good. Just don't forget you promised to take Ruby out to see the city at sunset. It's her last chance.'

And then she turned and walked down the corridor to her bedroom.

CHAPTER EIGHT

RUBY WAITED IN THE SALON in her carefully chosen outfit. She'd changed three times, veering between 'boating casual', which made her look as if she were going out for a country walk with her grandparents, and *Roman Holiday*, which made her look as if she was trying a little bit too hard. Maybe it had been the thick liquid liner and the red lipstick.

In the end she'd settled for a boat-necked navy cotton dress with a full enough skirt for clambering, her ballet pumps and a little black cardigan. The eyeliner stayed, but the lipstick was replaced by something in a more natural colour. Something that didn't scream 'Come and get me!', because she had a feeling there was no way Max was going to, even if it did.

While he hadn't answered the question she'd wanted to ask last night in words, his actions had done a pretty effective job for him. He wasn't in the grip of the same fairy-tale crush she had been, that was for sure.

If he had been, he wouldn't have avoided her all day. He certainly wouldn't have taken Sofia out for ice cream on his own that morning, saying that even trainee travelling nannies needed some time off. She knew a brush-off when she heard one. She'd been getting them from her father all her life.

She checked the ornate gold clock on the marble mantelpiece. Ten to seven. Fina had decreed they should leave here on the hour to catch the whole glory of the sunset, which was supposed to be closer to eight.

She wandered over to the long windows and took in the golden light hitting the front of a pink and white palazzo on the other side of the canal. Max had been right. This city spun a spell, making you believe things that weren't real, making you hope for things that could never be. She understood why so many people loved it now. And why he hated it.

She stayed there, watching the light play on the water, for what seemed like only a few minutes, and Fina startled her when she swept into the room and turned on the light. Ruby hadn't re-alised it had got that dark yet.

'Where's Max?' Fina asked, looking round, her brows drawn together.

Ruby shrugged. 'I don't know. We're supposed to be leaving at—'

The clock on the mantelpiece caught her eye. It was five past seven. He'd be here soon, though, she didn't doubt that. Whatever else Max was, he was a man of his word.

She almost wished he weren't. It was going to be awkward. She'd back out if she could, but she sensed Fina would blame Max somehow if she did, and the last thing Ruby wanted was to cause more trouble between mother and son.

Fina tutted and swept from the room before Ruby could say anything else.

Ruby walked over to an armchair at the edge of the seating area and dropped into it. It was one of those old seats that accepted her weight with a 'poof' then slowly sank until her bottom rested fully against the cushion.

She stared into the empty fireplace and waited. A few moments later she heard Fina clip-clop-ping back up the corridor. She entered the room and sighed dramatically. 'He has a very important phone call, apparently. The whole of London will fall down if he doesn't speak to this man at this precise minute.' She shook her head. 'I shall go and read to Sofia, but he says he will be out in only a few minutes.'

Ruby nodded, and placed her hands in her lap. She rested back against the armchair instead of sitting up poker straight. No point in getting a stiff back waiting for him.

There was a squeal and the sound of two pairs of footsteps—one small and slippered, the other bigger and harder—and a moment later Sofia ran into the room in her pyjamas, her grandmother in hot pursuit. She launched herself at Ruby and landed on her lap.

Fina pressed a hand to her chest, and said breathlessly, 'She's full of beans tonight, and she wanted to come and see you.'

'That's okay.' Then she turned to Sofia. 'Perhaps doing something quiet together for a few minutes will help you get ready for bed. What do you say, young lady?'

'Daw!' said Sofia loudly and pointed to the crayons and scrap paper that had been left out after their earlier colouring session.

Ruby chuckled and let Sofia slip off her lap before she joined her kneeling by the coffee table. 'And what would you like to draw this evening?'

Sofia thought for a moment. 'Naughty fish!'

Of course.

Ruby couldn't remember how many mischievous crabs she'd sketched since that first one: on the bottom of the lagoon, in a carnival mask, and Sofia's favourite—clinging determinedly to her uncle's big toe with a pair of razor-sharp pincers. She quickly did an outline in black pen, a gentler scene this time, something more in keeping with bedtime. She drew the cheeky crab in the back of a gondola with his equally cheeky crustacean girlfriend, being punted along by a singing gondolier in the moonlight.

When she realised what she'd done, how romantic she'd made the scene, she sighed and pushed it her charge's way.

There Venice went again…messing with her head.

'Here you go. And make sure you colour nicely. I don't want it all scribbled over in two seconds flat.'

Sofia nodded seriously, then set to work giving the lady crab a shock of purple hair, which Ruby approved of most heartily.

The sun was down behind the buildings now. Ruby stood and walked to the window, drawn closer by a patchwork sky of yellows and pinks and tangerines, sparsely smeared with silvery blue clouds. Venice, which often had an oddly monochrome feel to its palette, was bathed in golden light.

She walked back over to where Sofia was colouring and complimented her on her hard work, even though the cartoonish drawing she'd provided her with was almost entirely obliterated with heavy strokes of multicoloured crayon. She pulled out a piece of paper for herself. Most of the sheets had writing on the back. They'd gone through Fina's meagre stash of drawing paper and now were wading through documents Max had discarded, using them as scrap. Ruby flipped it over and looked at what was on the printed side.

It was a detail for an interior arch in one of the galleries of the National Institute of Fine Art. The shape was square with no adornment, and Ruby could see where the metal and studs of a supporting girder were left unhidden, giving it a textured, yet industrial air. She thought of the buildings Max had shown her up and down the canal, how he'd explained the Venetians had taken styles from the countries they visited with their own to make something unique, and, instead of turning the sheet back over again and drawing another princess, she picked up a pen and began to embellish.

She sighed, her heart heavy inside her chest. She might as well occupy herself while she waited.

'You need to get back here right away,' Alex, Max's second-in-command at Martin & Martin insisted, more than a hint of urgency in his tone.

Max closed his eyes to block out the dancing cherubs above his head. He'd been pacing to and fro in his mother's library and he was starting to get the uncanny feeling they were watching him. 'I know.'

'Vince McDermot wants the institute commission and he wants it bad.'

Max opened his eyes and stared at the screen on his laptop. 'I know. But the institute board have committed to giving me this extra few weeks to tweak our designs. They won't go back on that.'

Alex sighed. 'True, but McDermot has been out and about wining and dining key members of the board behind our backs. Either you need to come back to London and start schmoozing this instant or we need to come up with a design that'll blow that slimy little poser out of the water.'

Max knew this. He also knew he wasn't good at schmoozing. 'You're better at buttering clients up than I am.'

Alex let out a low, gruff laugh. 'Damn right, but it's you they want, Max. It's time to stop playing happy families and get your butt back here.'

Now it was Max's turn to laugh. *Happy families? Yeah, right.*

'I've been doing what needs to be done to focus on the work, Al. You know that.'

Alex grunted. 'All I'm saying is that there's no point in us burying our heads in the sand about this. Otherwise, the month will be up, we'll submit new designs and, even if they do have the "wow factor", the board will be more inclined to go with that flash-in-the-pan pretty boy.'

One of the reasons Max liked Alex, both as a colleague and a friend, was that he didn't mince his words. Alex had a point, though. Vince McDermot was London's new architectural wunderkind. Personally, Max thought his designs impractical and crowd-pleasing. They'd never stand the test of time.

'I'm flying back to London tomorrow afternoon, so that's that sorted,' he told Alex. 'The other stuff? Well, that's another story, but if we can keep them sweet for the next fortnight, it'll give us time to come up with what they're looking for.'

It had to come at some point, didn't it? He'd been hailed for his 'ground-breaking minimalist and elegant style', won awards for it. But that had been before. Now he couldn't come up with anything fresh and exciting. It was as if his talent had been buried with his father.

Alex made a conciliatory noise. 'Listen, I should have more of an idea of who exactly he's been sliming up to in the next fifteen minutes. Do you want me to call back, or are you going to hold?'

Max looked at the clock. It was half past seven.

He hadn't forgotten what that meant.

He was late. Really late.

'I'll hold,' he said.

His conscience grumbled. He let the relief flooding through him drown it out.

It was better this way. It was getting harder and harder to remember Ruby was his employee. Harder and harder to stop himself relaxing so much in her presence that he kept letting his guard down. He couldn't afford to do that. Not here. Not with his mother so close.

Better to put a stop to it now.

So Max made himself sit down. He made himself tinker with the designs for the institute's atrium. He made himself ignore the clawing feeling deep inside that told him he was being a heel, that he was hurting her for no reason.

Unfortunately, he didn't do a very good job of it. Probably because the lines and angles in front of him on the screen kept going out of focus, and he kept imagining what it would be like to be out in the boat with Ruby, the dark wrapping around them, enclosing them in their own little bubble while the lights of the city danced on the lagoon.

That only made him crosser.

Damn her. It was all her fault, waltzing into his neatly ordered life, turning it upside down.

You asked her. Hell, you practically commanded her to come with you.

Yeah? Well, everybody made mistakes. Even him. Occasionally.

It was only when he stood up to pace around the room again that he realised he'd put the phone down on Alex at some point in the last five minutes and hadn't even noticed. He said a word that should have made the cherubs on the ceiling put their fingers in their ears.

And all that messing around he'd done on the atrium plans was a load of rubbish! In fact, all the work he'd done on them in the last couple of days had been tired and uninspiring. What had he been thinking?

He shook his head, perfectly aware of what had been filling it. That was why it would be so much better when he was back in London. He'd be able to get his brain round it then, removed from any distractions. Any strawberry-clad, purple-streaked distractions.

Now, where was the earlier atrium design? The one where he'd pared it all back to the basics? He might as well get rid of all these silly changes and start from scratch.

He rummaged through the papers on his mother's antique desk. He'd had a printout of it. It had to be around here somewhere.

Ruby sat back on her heels and surveyed her handiwork. Not bad, even if she did say so herself. Maybe Max was right about her having some real artistic flair. Maybe she could do something with it, rather than just 'messing around', as her father called it.

There was such beauty and simplicity in Max's designs, but this one had just needed a little something—a curve here, a twirl there. By the time she'd finished, the arch on Max's discarded plan was a strange hybrid between twenty-first-century industrial and Venetian Gothic, with a little bit of Ruby thrown in for fun.

Perhaps she should be an architect?

The fact she didn't burst out laughing then roll on the floor at that thought was all thanks to Max. He'd believed in her ability to draw, seen something no one else saw, and she was starting to think she could even see it herself. She wanted to tell him that when they went out later, to thank him, but she didn't really know how to put it into words without betraying everything else she was starting to feel.

'More fish!' Sofia demanded, grinning at Ruby so appealingly that Ruby didn't have the heart to make her say please.

'I think maybe it's time Grandma tucked you into bed,' she told Sofia, smiling. Fina rose from where she'd been reading a magazine in an armchair, and held her hand out for her granddaughter. After running and giving Ruby a hug, Sofia allowed herself to be led away and Ruby was once again alone in the salon.

She tried not to look, but the gold clock on the mantelpiece drew her gaze like a magnet.

Eight o'clock.

A quick glance outside confirmed her suspicions. Compared to the brightly lit salon, the sky outside was bottomless and dark. Not helped by the heavy clouds that had started to gather over the city in the last half hour.

Max had stood her up.

She let her eyelids rest gently closed and inhaled. It didn't matter.

The heaviness in her heart called her a liar.

But it shouldn't be there. She was a paid employee. He owed her nothing more than her wages.

It was just…

She shook her head and opened her eyes again, then she got off up the floor and started piling the scattered bits of drawing up, putting the crayons back in their tub.

Just nothing.

She'd been fooling herself again, thinking this was something when it wasn't. Max hadn't seen inside her, he hadn't spotted the potential that no one else had. He'd just paid her a compliment or two, that was all. And that kiss? Heat-of-the-moment stuff that produced nothing but regrets. She'd doled out a few of those herself in her time. Nothing to sweat about.

Then why did she feel like going to her room, shutting the door behind her and bawling her eyes out?

She gathered the sheets of paper in various sizes up in her arms and headed towards the door. She wasn't quite sure where she was going to put these, but she suspected Fina wouldn't want them scattered around her most formal living space. Maybe they could find a home for one or two of the best ones on the fridge door?

She couldn't have been looking where she'd been going, because when the salon door burst open and Max came barrelling through she didn't have time for evasive manoeuvres. She stumbled sideways, the stack of paper went flying into the air and then fluttered noisily down like oversized confetti.

Max just stood in the doorway, looking somewhat stunned.

He didn't say anything, but he shook himself

slightly then bent to help her pick up the scattered drawings.

Damn him for being such a gentleman. She wanted to hate him right now.

'Here,' he said, when they'd finished gathering up the last of them, and held a sheaf of papers in her direction.

'Thanks,' she mumbled, chickening out of looking him in the eye.

Max must have been doing the same, because suddenly he got very interested in the top sheet of paper.

'What the hell?' he started to say, and then his expression grew thunderous. 'What's this?'

Ruby rolled her eyes. 'Sorry,' she said, feeling her cheeks heat. 'I didn't intend to make the cartoon of you being bitten by the crab at first, but Sofia thought it looked like you, because it was a man, probably, and then it just became a kind of joke and we—'

'I'm not talking about a silly drawing!' Max said, his voice getter louder.

His words were like a punch to Ruby's gut. 'But I—'

'I'm talking about *this*!' And he thrust a sheet of paper so close to her face that she had to step back to focus on it. It was the doodle she'd just finished: Max's arch with her little bit of decorative nonsense superimposed.

Artist? Hah! Don't kid yourself, Ruby.

'It was just… I mean, I just…' She let out a frustrated sigh and spiked her fingers through her neatly combed fringe. 'It's just a doodle, Max.'

'A *doodle*?'

Ruby's heart thudded and her stomach dived into her ballet pumps. If the heat of Max's anger hadn't been scalding her face, his expression would have been kind of funny. She nodded, feeling all the while that she was walking into an ambush that she didn't know how to avoid.

'These are my plans!' Max bellowed. 'What on earth makes you think you have the right to *doodle* on them? Are you out of your mind?'

Ruby's mouth moved and she backed away. 'But, it was there…' her gaze flicked to the coffee table, where the pile of unmolested scrap paper still sat. '…with the stuff you tossed out the other day…on the top of the pile.'

'This wasn't *scrap*!' he yelled. 'These are my original plans. You had no right to use them for Sofia. No right at all.'

Ruby was so puzzled that she couldn't even

react to Max's anger at that moment. How had Max's plans got there? How? He'd given them the sheaf of papers himself yesterday and, okay, she hadn't noticed that one sitting on top then, but neither she nor Sofia had been anywhere near the library. The plans couldn't have walked here on their own.

'I don't understand,' she said, shaking her head.

Max began to laugh. But it wasn't the warm, rich sound she remembered from the the day they'd gone crabbing. It was a dark, rasping sound that made the hair on her arms stand up on end.

'Of course,' he said, shaking his head. 'I knew I shouldn't have hired you. Why I didn't listen to my gut I'll never know. What was I thinking? You have no qualifications, no experience—'

Now was the moment that the furnace of Ruby's anger decided to *whomph* into life. She went from shivery and cold to raging inferno in the space of a heartbeat.

'You're right!' she yelled back at him. 'You want to know if I'm cut out to be a nanny? Well, I can answer that right now—I'm not! Not if it means I have to like working for closed-off, emotionally constipated jerks like you.'

Max went very still and his expression was completely neutral. If anything, that was more worrying than all the bluff and fluster had been. Ruby felt herself start to shake. She knew she'd gone too far, that she shouldn't have said that. But, as the sensible side of her brain tried to tell her that, the impulsive, emotional side blocked its ears and sang *la la la*.

'I should fire you for this,' he said, and his voice was as cold as the marble floor beneath their feet.

'Don't bother,' she shot back, making enough heat and anger for both of them. 'I quit. I'm not cut out for this and I don't want to be.' And she dumped the pile of paper she'd been holding onto Max's pile and stomped off towards the door. Thank goodness she only had that one rucksack to pack. She could be out of here within the hour.

'That's right,' Max said, his voice low and infuriatingly even as she reached the door. 'Run out on another job.'

She spun round to face him. 'You know nothing about me. So don't you dare judge me.'

He stared her down. The fire from a few moments earlier was gone, doused by a healthy dollop of concrete, if his expression was anything to go by.

'I know that you bail when the going gets tough, that you've never seen a single job through to the end.'

'So? That's my business, not yours. You've made that abundantly clear.'

He stepped forward. 'I'm afraid it is my business when you're leaving before the end of your contract.'

That was when Ruby smiled. She really shouldn't, but it started somewhere deep down inside and bubbled up until it reached her lips. 'And there's your problem, Mr Hot Shot. I don't have a contract, remember?'

And, leaving him to chew on that, she stalked down the corridor. Pity she was wearing ballet slippers, because it would have been so much more effective in heels.

'We had a verbal agreement!' he yelled after her.

Ruby's response was to keep walking but use some non-verbal communication she was pretty sure was offensive in just about any language you cared to mention.

An angry shudder ripped through her as she headed for her room, already mentally packing her rucksack. And she'd thought she was attracted to this man? She really was insane. The sooner she got out of Venice, the better.

CHAPTER NINE

MAX WAS SO FURIOUS he couldn't speak, could hardly even breathe. How dare she act as if he were in the wrong? And how dare she bail on him after only one week? What was he going to do now? Knowing his mother, she'd make an impulsive decision and say she couldn't possibly keep Sofia here on her own, and then he'd be stuck here, right when it was more urgent than ever that he leave this tangled family mess behind and concentrate even harder on his work.

He wanted to march after Ruby, to give her a piece of his mind, but he suspected she was in no mood to listen. She was stubborn as hell, that woman, and bound to dig her heels in if he went in with all guns blazing.

He'd give her half an hour. Then he'd go and find her, make her see sense.

He looked down at the stack of papers in his hands. His scribbled-on plans were on top. Just the sight of them made his temperature rise a couple of notches. He turned and headed for the library. At least he'd be able to distract himself for a short while trying to see if anything was salvageable. Once he was there, he dropped the stack of papers on the desk and sank into the chair.

It had to have been her fault. She must have come and got more paper from his makeshift office at some point, despite what she'd said, because how else could his pristine plans have ended up on Sofia's drawing-paper pile? They hadn't been outside the library all week.

A cold feeling washed through him from head to toe.

Except…

Last night, when he'd taken some papers into the salon as a cure for insomnia, and the plans had been amongst them. It had worked, too. After an hour and a half of poring over them, going over every detail, he'd woken himself up, his head lolling against his chest, and then he'd stumbled back to bed.

Oh, hell.

And he had no idea if he'd stumbled back into the library first and replaced the plans.

He stared at the clean, narrow printed-out lines of his plans, with Ruby's thicker doodlings over the top. It was his fault, wasn't it? Not hers. While he hadn't exactly put them on Sofia's paper stack by leaving them lying around in the salon he'd opened up the way for them to get muddled into it during the course of the day.

Max exhaled heavily and let his forehead drop so it rested on the pile of papers.

Damn.

And he'd lost his temper. Something he never did. He'd always hated losing control like that. Not just because when his really long fuse went, it tended to verge on apocalyptic, but because of how he was feeling right now. Raw. Open. Weak.

If it had been Sofia that had done the drawing he knew he wouldn't have reacted the same way. Oh, he'd have been cross, but he wouldn't have exploded like that, and not just because she was only two and he would have scared the living daylights out of her.

There was something about Ruby that just got under his skin.

He sat up, ran his hand through his hair and stared at the dark green wallpaper.

He should let her leave, shouldn't he?

She wanted to. It would certainly be better for him.

But he needed her.

He shook his head. No. He didn't need any-one. Especially not a woman who ran at the first sniff of trouble, which was exactly what Ruby had done, proving his point very nicely for him.

He needed a nanny. That was all.

The choice was up to her. If she still wanted to go he wouldn't stop her, but there was one thing he needed to do first—apologise.

In a bit, though. Ruby was probably still spit-ting fire, and if he tried to knock on her door now, he'd probably get a few more of those wonderfully eloquent hand gestures.

A smile crept across his face, even though he knew it wasn't really funny at all.

She was a pill, that one.

He sighed and turned his attention back to the plans in front of him, unfolding the paper and having a good look. It was interesting what she'd drawn. She'd taken his plain, square arch and added some traditional Venetian style to it. She really had been paying attention to the shapes and patterns of the buildings, hadn't she? Here was an ogee arch, and here a lobed one. She'd re-produced them perfectly, even when she'd only been doodling.

That was when something smacked him straight between the eyebrows.

The shapes.

Ruby had been talking about the geometric shapes, the other day, the way simple ones interlocked to make more complicated ones. All he'd been able to see when he came to Venice was the fuss, the frilliness. He'd forgotten that even the most of ornate fasciae were constructed of much simpler, cleaner elements.

If he took Ruby's idea and pared it back, using simpler shapes, overlapping and juxtaposing them to create something, not exactly elaborate, because that wasn't his style, but something more intricate that still kept that essence of simple elegance.

He grabbed one of Sofia's scrap-paper sheets and a pen and began to scribble. Semicircular arches here and here, intersecting to create a more pointed version, with slender pillar for support. His hand flew over the paper, sketching shapes and lines, at first for the arches in the atrium, but then taking the same idea and applying it to other aspects of the space, giving it all a cohesive feel.

He could see it so clearly. Just a hint of gothic style, built in glass and steel. Modern materials that echoed back to classic design. It was just what he needed to tie the new wing and the existing institute building together and make them feel like one space.

He kept going, filling sheet after sheet, until he suddenly realised he'd been at this for ages.

Ruby!

He still hadn't gone and apologised.

He shoved away from the desk, sending a stack of Sofia's colourful drawings flying, and then sprinted down the corridor in the direction of her and Ruby's rooms. He didn't bother knocking when he got there, just flung the door open and raced inside, expecting to find her shoving clothes into her rucksack, a scowl on her face.

Wrong again, Max.

She can pack in under ten minutes, remember? Sometimes five.

Where Max had expected to find Ruby stewing and muttering insults under her breath, there was nothing but empty space.

Ruby Lange was gone.

Ruby shivered as she waited on the little creaky dock outside Ca' Damiani. The clouds had sunk closer to the water and coloured everything a murky grey. A drop of rain splashed on her forehead. Great.

Her rucksack was at her feet, leaning against her lower legs, and she craned to see if the light bobbing towards her, accompanied by the sound of a motor, was the taxi she'd ordered. She needed to get out of here and she needed to do it right now.

This was so *not* how she'd imagined seeing Venice by water this evening.

More raindrops, one after the other. She could hear them plopping into the canal near her feet.

The approaching craft turned out to be a private boat that puttered past and stopped outside one of the buildings opposite. Ruby felt her whole body sag.

Stupid, stupid girl. You take on a job you know nothing about—just because some random guy says he needs you—and you think he's going to see past all of your inexperience and believe you're something special? Get real. The only thing Max Martin believed about her was that she was a flaky screw-up, just like everyone else on this planet.

She hugged her arms tighter around her, wishing she hadn't packed her jacket in the very bottom of the rucksack.

Not everyone believes you're a screw-up.

Okay, maybe she was being a little dramatic. A number of her bosses over the years had begged her to stay when she'd realised the job wasn't for her and had given in her notice. They'd said she was competent and organised and they'd love to promote her, but she hadn't been able to ignore that itchy feeling once it started. The only way to stop the intense restlessness, the only way to scratch it enough so it went away, was to move on. But Max was wrong. She didn't run away. She ran *to* the next thing. There was a whole world of difference.

The rain began to fall harder now. She pushed her fringe out of her eyes. It was already damp. Where *was* that taxi?

There was a creaking behind her as the boat door that led to the dock opened. Ruby's blood solidified in her veins. She refused to turn round.

She expected another angry tirade, braced herself against it, but when his voice came it was soft and low. 'Ruby?'

'That's my name,' she said, and then grimaced,

glad he couldn't see her face. What was this? High school?

'Don't go.'

She spun round to face him, arms still clutched around her middle, as if she was afraid she'd fall apart if she didn't hold herself together. 'What?'

The anger was gone. She could see none of its vestiges on his features. Part of her breathed a sigh of relief, but another, deeper part, sighed with disappointment. The anger had been horrible, but it had been a little wonderful, too.

He walked forwards. Ruby was tempted to back away, but that would mean taking a dip in the canal, so she had to stay where she was. Cold drops peppered her skin and she shivered. Off in the distance there was a muffled rumble of thunder.

'I want to apologise,' he said, looking so earnest her heart grew warm and achy inside her chest. 'I should never have let off at you like that. It was totally uncalled for.'

'Thank you,' she said in a wobbly voice. 'And I should probably apologise for the verbal—and non-verbal—assault. That wasn't very professional.'

A wry smile lifted one corner of his mouth. 'I deserved it.'

Her stony blood started to warm and melt. It danced and shimmered and sang. *Stop it*, she told it. *You're making it very hard to leave.*

And so was he, looking at her like that.

The itchy feeling returned, stronger this time. Unable to stand still, she walked in a small circle. The falling rain multiplied the lights of the city, but a cold breeze wrapped around her, stealing her breath.

'It was my fault the plans got mixed up with Sofia's drawing paper,' he said, not breaking eye contact. 'I left them in the salon the night before. I'm sorry I accused you of that.'

She nodded, not trusting herself to say anything.

He looked down at his feet briefly before meeting her eyes again. 'Forgive me.'

Revenge, passion and utter, utter devotion. The words spun through Ruby's head.

'Okay,' she croaked.

He nodded, his expression still slightly grim. 'Then stay…please?'

Ruby blinked. Up until now, she hadn't been sure that word was part of Max Martin's vocabulary.

She looked away, even closed her eyes for good measure. She'd wanted to go so badly. So badly… It was a surprise to discover the tug to stay was just as strong. Not to stay and be Sofia's nanny, although she was sure she would enjoy another week of that, but to stay here. In Venice. With Max.

She sucked a breath in and held it. Thank goodness he had no idea about the silly things she'd been feeling. Thank goodness he probably thought she was acting out of hurt pride. And fear, yes. He'd been right about that. She did run when things got too hard. Always had. How could you save yourself the crushing pain of disappointment otherwise?

She opened her eyes and looked out across the water. The moon was rising farther away, where the clouds had not yet blotted it out. It cast a silvery glow on the far-off bell towers and roofs, spilling glitter on the still waters of this back canal, where it undulated softly. It looked like a fairy tale.

And if this were a fairy tale, she'd stay. Max would fall madly in love with her and make her his princess. In their happy-ever-after she'd soothe his pain, teach him to let it go, and they'd be gloriously happy together.

Only real life didn't work that way. It hadn't for her and her father, and it hadn't for Fina. Only a fool wouldn't escape when they had the chance rather than sentence themselves to that kind of misery.

If she stayed, she might fall for him properly, not just teeter on the brink of an *inappropriate* crush.

She pulled her rucksack up from the floor of the dock and hugged it to her before turning to face him. 'I don't know, Max. I don't think it's a good idea I stay…for anybody.'

The water taxi chose that moment to turn up. The driver, oblivious to the tense scene occurring on the little wooden dock, looped a rope round a post and called out in Italian.

Ruby wiped the rain off her face and waved to show she'd heard him, then she slipped the straps of her rucksack over her shoulders. She pressed her lips together and tried not to let her eyes shimmer. 'Goodbye. Tell Fina and Sofia I'm sorry.' And then she turned and steadied herself before stepping into the boat.

As she lifted her foot he called out again. 'Don't go.'

She turned to look over her shoulder. 'Why, Max? Why shouldn't I go?'

For a moment he didn't say anything, but then he looked her straight in the eye. 'Because I need you.'

CHAPTER TEN

IF RUBY HAD THOUGHT she'd felt a little breathless before, now she really struggled to pull oxygen into her body. Max needed her?

He doesn't mean it that way. Don't be stupid.

'No, you just need a proper nanny. It isn't me *specifically* that you need.'

No words left Max's mouth, but she discovered his eyes contradicted her quite beautifully. Her heart literally stopped beating inside her chest, just for a second. When it started up again, her pulse thundered in her ears.

She let her rucksack slip off her shoulders and it landed behind her on the dock with a thud. The rain began to fall in earnest, soaking the thin wool of her cardigan, but she didn't seem to feel the damp and cold seeping into her skin.

Him, too? It hadn't just been a physical, knee-jerk kind of thing?

That made her feel as if the world had just done a somersault around her and she needed to find solid ground again. Pity she was stranded in a city where that was in short supply.

That didn't mean she was about to commit emotional suicide by staying, though. She cleared her throat. 'I meant what I said earlier, Max. I don't think I'm cut out to be a nanny in the long term.'

He nodded. 'I agree. But I'm not asking you to be a nanny for the rest of your life. I'm just asking you to be one for the next week or so. After that it's up to you.'

She nodded. That all sounded very sensible.

'If you don't think I'm cut out to be a nanny, why on earth do you want me to stay and look after Sofia?'

Max gave her a weary look. 'I didn't say I didn't think you could do the job.' He smiled gently. 'I said it because I didn't think you should commit yourself to something when your talent clearly lies elsewhere.'

Ruby's eyes widened. 'You think I have talent?'

He frowned. 'Don't *you*? Your drawings are fabulous, and that doodle you did on my plans set ideas firing off in my head so fast I could hardly keep up with them.' The smile grew into a grin. 'I have my "wow factor" for the Institute now, Ruby, and it's all because of you.'

She closed her eyes and opened them again, not quite able to believe what she was hearing. 'Do you... Do you think I should be an architect?'

His eyes warmed, making her forget the salty lagoon breeze that kept lifting the shorter bits of her hair now and then. 'I think you could do that if you wanted to, but there's something about your sketches that's so full of life and personality. I think you've got something there. They're quirky and original and full of...'

You. His eyes must have said that bit, because his mouth had stopped moving.

'They're captivating.'

Ruby felt the echo of his words rumble deep down inside her. Or maybe it was the crack of thunder that shook the sky over their heads.

Oh, heck. She really was in trouble, wasn't she? How could she leave now?

And maybe Max was right. Maybe it was time to stop running. She might not have to see being a nanny through to the bitter end, but she could see this job through. How could she leave them all in the lurch like this? Sofia wouldn't understand where she'd gone and feel abandoned all over again, Fina would be saddled with looking after a toddler full time, and Max wouldn't have time to work on his plans, and she really wanted him to do that.

She still didn't believe there was much in the future for them, even if some bizarre chemistry was popping between them, but she'd like to visit the National Institute of Fine Art on a rainy afternoon in a few years' time and sit under Max's atrium and feel happy—and maybe a little sad—to know that she'd had something to do with it, that in some lasting way she had a tiny connection to him.

She looked down at the rucksack threatening to pitch off the dock and into the canal. The taxi driver, whom she'd forgotten all about, coughed and mumbled something grumpily about being made to hang about in this kind of weather. She shot him a look of desperation.

He shrugged in that fatalistic Italian way, his expression saying, *Are you coming or not?*

Ruby looked back at Max. He was waiting. Not shouting. Not bulldozering. It was totally her choice and she knew he would hold no grudges if she got on this boat and told the driver to take her to the Piazzale Roma to catch a train.

She swallowed and twisted to face the driver

and rummaged in her pocket and gave him a tip for his trouble. *'Mi dispiace, signore.'*

Ruby woke up to sunshine pouring into her bedroom the next morning. She stumbled over to the window, which overlooked a narrow little canal that ran down the side of the palazzo. It almost felt as if the night before had never happened. There was no hint of the storm. The sky was the clear pale blue of a baby's blanket, hardly a cloud to mar it, and where the sun hit the canal it was a fierce and glittering emerald.

Things were just as surreal at breakfast, with Fina bustling around and fussing over Sofia, never once mentioning that Ruby had packed her bags and tried to leave last night.

Max had been in the library since before she'd got up, and that had been pretty early. She half expected him to bury himself away all day, working on his plans until it was time to pack up and leave for the airport. She didn't know what would be worse: not seeing him most of the day or spending a bittersweet last few hours with him before he returned to London. She'd forgotten all about that last night when she'd agreed to stay. So when the salon door opened at ten o'clock and Max walked in, Ruby's heart leapt and cowered at the same time.

'What do you want to do this morning?' he asked his niece, glancing briefly at Ruby and giving a nod of greeting.

'Fishing!' Sofia yelled and ran off in the direction of the cupboard where the crabbing gear was kept.

Both Ruby and Max charged after her, knowing just how tightly that cupboard was packed and just how much mischief an unattended two-year-old could get up to inside it. They managed to beat Sofia to the lines and hooks, but Max gave her a bucket and a small net to carry to keep her happy. And then they bustled around, getting into the boat, coaxing Sofia into a life jacket, making sure she didn't let go of her bucket and leave it floating down a canal somewhere.

She and Max worked as a team, exchanging words when needed, passing equipment to each other, but it wasn't until they were standing at Max's favourite crabbing spot, the little boat moored up and bobbing about a short distance away, that they slowed down enough for Ruby to get a sense of his mood.

She watched him gently helping Sofia wind an

empty line back up without getting it tangled. He'd been polite this morning, almost friendly.

Had she imagined it? Had it all been some weird dream, a spell cast by this contrary city?

She let out a long sigh. Maybe it was better if that was the case. It was sheer craziness. Even if she'd seen what she'd thought she'd seen in his eyes last night, what did she think was going to happen? A wild fling in his mother's house, with a toddler running around?

Once again, get real, Ruby.

She knelt down and took interest in what Sofia was doing. She'd plopped the crab line into the water for the fourth or fifth time, but so far no luck. The little girl heaved out a sigh. 'Fish go 'way,' she said slightly despondently.

Ruby couldn't help but smile. Despite her self-contained manner, Sofia had a little bit of her grandmother's flair for drama in her. She forgot herself, looked up at Max to share the joke. He was crouching the other side of Sofia, who was sitting on the edge of the *fondamenta* where the railings parted, her little legs swinging above the water, and their eyes met across the top of her head.

Ruby almost fell in the canal.

It was all there, everything he hadn't said last night and everything he had.

Oh, heck. Just when she'd almost managed to talk some sense into herself.

And it still all did make sense. He was her boss. He was going back to London in a matter of hours. He was her total polar opposite. In what world was that anything but a recipe for disaster?

Everywhere but Venice, she discovered as a slow smile spread across her lips. She felt she must be glowing. Actually radiating something. It would probably scare the fish away.

She wanted to lean across, press her lips to his, wind her arms around his neck and just taste him. Feel him. Dive into him.

'Fish!' Sofia yelled, and it was almost her who did the diving. She got so excited she almost toppled off the edge into the canal. It was only Max's quick reflexes that saved her.

After that they made sure they had their eyes on Sofia instead of each other at all times. It didn't matter, though. It was pulsing in the air around them, like a wonderful secret, a song carried on a radio wave that only they could tune into.

She felt it as they ended their crabbing expedition, a weary Sofia rubbing her eyes and complaining about being hungry. She felt it as they stood mere inches apart at the front of the boat, Max steering, her holding Sofia so she could see over the top of the little motorboat's windscreen. Felt it as they passed buckets and nets and bags to each other from boat to dry land.

As they pulled the last of the luggage from the boat and headed into the large downstairs hall of the palazzo Ruby turned to Max, made proper eye contact in what seemed the first time in decades. 'What time's your flight?' she asked, plainly and simply.

It was all very well dreaming on the canals, but their feet were back on solid ground now. It was time to anchor herself back in reality, remind herself of what really was happening here.

'Five o'clock,' he said.

She nodded towards the first floor. 'You'd better get going if you're going to get any work done before you have to stop and pack.' She held out her hand to take the nets from him.

Max looked at her for a long while, and an ache started low down in her belly. 'Yes,' he said, and then handed her the nets and set off up the staircase, taking the steps two at a time.

* * *

Ruby jiggled her leg while she waited for Sofia to finish brushing her teeth. Once she'd had a try herself, Ruby dived in and gave them another going-over. As mundane as the task was, she was glad of something to do. Sofia had had an extra-long sleep that afternoon. Ruby had gone into her room again and again, expecting to find her jumping on the bed, but each time Sofia had been sprawled on the mattress, her pink rabbit tucked in the crook of her arm and her thumb in her mouth.

She'd heard Max leave the palazzo around three. His plane was probably somewhere over the English Channel now.

He hadn't even said goodbye.

A stab of something hit her in the stomach, but she forced it away. She bundled Sofia from the bathroom and back to her bedroom, where she found Fina sitting on the bed, waiting for them.

'You are looking tired, *piccola*.'

Ruby ruffled Sofia's hair. 'I don't know why, after that mammoth sleep she had.'

Fina smiled and tipped her head on one side. 'I was talking about you, my darling.'

Ruby tried not to react. Was it really that obvious?

Fina waved her hand in a regal manner. 'Well,

it is all for the good. I came to say I would read Sofia her story and put her to bed tonight, so you go and relax in the salon.'

Ruby shook her head. More sitting around with nothing to do—the last thing she needed. 'It's my job, Fina—'

Fina stopped her with an imperious eyebrow lift. 'But I wish to. So…off you go.' And she dismissed Ruby with a gracious smile.

There wasn't much Ruby could say to that, so she sloped off in the direction of the salon to do as she was told. The setting sun was streaming in through the windows when she entered the room, almost blinding her, and at first she didn't see the dark shape by the window, but after a moment or two the dark smudge morphed into something more solid.

Ruby's mouth dropped open. 'B-but I thought you were going back to London!'

Max turned round. He was silhouetted against the ornate arches, and she couldn't see his face, let alone read his features.

'So did I.'

She shook her head. 'What changed?'

'Nothing…and everything.'

He stepped forward out of the light and Ruby

could see he wasn't wearing his suit, just dark casual trousers and a light sweater. Her heart began to beat faster.

'But this afternoon, when I carried on using the ideas from your doodle and incorporating a pared-down Venetian style into my plans for the institute, I realised I need to be here, not in London. I need to get my inspiration from the source, not just inaccurate and misleading memories. I've spent all afternoon wandering around looking at buildings I've known all my life and seeing them with completely fresh eyes.' He shook his head.

Ruby glanced over her shoulder towards the corridor, and Sofia's bedroom. She could just about hear the warm tones of Fina's voice as she read her granddaughter a fairy story. 'There's something to be said for stripping the preconceptions and prejudices of the past away and looking at things with fresh eyes.'

'Did my mother put you up to saying that?'

She turned back, expecting him to be scowling, but his face was almost neutral, save for the barest hint of a smile.

One corner of Ruby's mouth lifted. 'No. I think I'm quite capable of irritating you without outside help.'

Max laughed, and it made something rise like a balloon inside Ruby and bump against the ceiling of her ribs.

He walked towards the door in the path of a long, golden shadow. 'Come on,' he said.

Ruby frowned, but she turned to follow anyway. 'Where?'

He stopped and looked back at her. 'You missed seeing Venice at sunset last night because I had an attack of stupid. It's only right I should make it up to you tonight.'

CHAPTER ELEVEN

AS THEY WALKED along the little wooden dock in front of his mother's palazzo, Max couldn't help but remember being there with Ruby the night before. He jumped down into the little speedboat, and Ruby followed him. Without even asking, she helped with the ropes and fenders.

She'd only been here a week, and no one had shown her what to do. She'd just picked it up, that quick mind of hers soaking up all the information and putting it effortlessly to use.

She sat in the stern as he drove the boat away, silent. The outfit tonight was the plainest one yet. No hippies. No rock chicks. No damn strawberries. All she wore was a cream blouse with soft ruffles, a pair of capris and a light cardigan thrown over her shoulders. He watched her drink in the way the setting sun made every façade richer and more glorious, harking back to the days when some had actually been covered entirely in gold leaf.

In fact, he found it hard to *stop* watching her. But he needed to.

Ruby Lange seemed bright and sunny and harmless, but she was a dangerous substance. She dissolved through his carefully constructed walls without even trying. He really should keep her at a distance.

Then why did you invite her to come out with you this evening?

Because it was the right thing to do. He'd acted like a total idiot the previous evening and so he was making it up to her. And he'd given his word. He'd said he'd show her Venice at sunset and so he was going to show her Venice at sunset.

Yeah, right. You keep telling yourself that. It has nothing to do with wanting to be alone with her, with wanting her to melt those walls that have left you claustrophobic and breathless for too long.

Max steered the boat down the canal and busied himself doing what he'd come here to do—no, not spend time alone with Ruby, but offer his services as tour guide and boat driver. He beckoned for her to come up and stand beside him, pointed out a few landmarks, and they talked easily about history and architecture for at least ten minutes.

It wasn't working.

Inside there was a timer counting down, ticking away the seconds until the sun slipped below the horizon and he and Ruby would be cocooned in the dark. He couldn't stop thinking about it.

He needed to remember why this was a bad idea, remember why Ruby wasn't right for him. As alluring as she might be, last night's uproar had proved one thing quite firmly: Ruby Lange ran when things got too close, when things got too serious. And these days he was nothing but serious.

He slowed the engine a little and looked over at her. 'Why do you move from job to job?'

She tore her gaze off the city and looked at him. 'I told you the other night. I want to find my perfect fit, like my father has. Like you have.'

He took his eyes off her for a moment to steer past a boat going a little slower than they were. 'Does it have to be perfect?'

Ruby gave him a puzzled smile. 'Well, I'd like it to be. Who wants to do a job their whole life if they have no passion for it?'

'Millions of people do.'

She shook her head. 'I want more out of life. I'm tired with settling for crumbs. I want the whole banquet.'

He nodded. That part he understood only too well, but there was something else she hadn't considered.

'Whatever my mother says, I wasn't sure about architecture, at least not when it came time to choose a profession,' he told her, returning his gaze to the canal, as they'd turned into a busier, wider stretch and he needed to pay attention, but every now and then he glanced over at her. 'I liked it. It fascinated me, but, like you, I wasn't sure it was what I wanted to do with my life. I often wondered if I'd picked it because I wanted to impress my father.'

On his next glance across her eyes were wide. 'It's not your passion?' she almost whispered. 'Because if it isn't, I'd be fascinated to see what you're like when you really get into something!'

He smiled. 'No. It is my passion, or at least it is now. What I'm trying to say is that what if there is no perfect job, not at the start? What if it's the learning, the discipline of immersing yourself in it and scaling the learning curves that makes it a perfect fit?'

She frowned and her eyes made tiny, rapid side-to-side movements as she worked that one out in her head. She frowned harder. He guessed she hadn't been able to neatly file that thought and shove it away out of sight.

'But how do you do that and not lose your heart and soul to something that might not be the right choice?' Her voice dropped to the scratchiest of whispers. 'What do you do if you choose something and it doesn't choose you back?'

He shrugged. Maybe he'd been lucky. 'But there's the irony—you may never know unless you try.'

She folded her arms, scowled and turned away to look at the buildings as he turned the boat onto the Grand Canal. 'That's a very Italian thing to say,' she muttered darkly.

'I *am* half Italian,' he reminded her.

She shot him a saucy look. 'And there was me, thinking you'd forgotten.'

Then she turned and just absorbed the scenery. They'd come from the relative quiet and muted tones of the smaller canals onto the wide strip of water that snaked through the centre of the city. Suddenly it was all light and colour.

Sunset seemed further away here, out of the shadows of the tall buildings, where the remaining light reflected off the water onto the palazzos and back into the sky. Awnings were pulled down over restaurants that lined the water's edge, and the spaces inside were bustling, full of warm light and moving people.

She looked across at him. 'Talking of trying, your mother is very pleased you're staying on.'

He gave her a resigned look. 'I know.'

'So why won't you let *her* try, Max?'

There she went again, tapping at his walls with her little pickaxe, testing them for weak spots.

'Have you ever listened to her side of the story?' she continued. 'Or have you always gone on what your father told you?'

Ouch.

She'd found one. A chink in his perception of his life that he hadn't even realised had been there. He tried to plug it up. 'I saw enough with my own eyes,' he replied gruffly. 'And my father rarely spoke of her.'

But the damage had been done. Memories started spilling into his brain, scenes of his parents' marriage. He'd always thought he'd understood what was going on so clearly, but it was as if this was another version of the same film, and different details sprang to life, tiny things that tipped everything on its head—the look of desperation in his mother's eyes, the way she'd sobbed late into the night, the way she'd looked at his father, with such adoration, in both good times and bad.

He drowned them out by taking another, busier route with the boat, so he had to give driving it his full concentration. He steered the boat down the canal and out towards St Mark's Square. It was full of gondolas of sighing tourists here, and he felt his irritation with the city, with its over-the-topness returning. Maybe Ruby had something in her idea of not wanting to give your heart and soul to something, only to be disappointed.

'Can *you* try?' she asked softly.

As always, she took what he was prepared to give and pushed him to cough up more. The sensation was one rather akin to having a particularly sticky plaster ripped off a tender patch of skin.

'And that's what happens in your family, is it?' He glanced skyward, noticing neither the pink drifting clouds nor the orange sky behind them. 'Last I heard, you were all for keeping parents at a safe distance.'

Ruby looked at her shoes. He couldn't see her cheeks, but he'd bet they were warmer than they'd been a few seconds ago. 'I didn't think you'd remember that,' she mumbled.

'Well, I did.' She could have been right, though.

He managed to tune out most people most of the time, but there was something about Ruby that made him listen, even when he'd dearly like to switch everything off and sink into blessed silence. 'So maybe you should practise what you preach before you start lecturing me.'

She shuffled her feet and looked up at him, arms still hugging herself. 'Okay, maybe I should. But I've tried over the years with my father, Max, and he always keeps me at arm's length, no matter what.'

That was hard to believe. Look at her, with her large, expressive eyes, her zest for life, which still seemed to be threatening to burst out of her, despite her slightly subdued mood. He was having trouble *maintaining* a distance of arm's length.

'Why?' he asked, glad for a chance to swing the interrogation light her way.

Ruby sat down on one of the cushioned benches. Max slowed the motor and brought the craft to a halt, letting it bob on the canal as the pleasure boats, *vaporetti* and gondolas drifted past. He turned to lean against the steering wheel and looked back at her.

She shook her head, staring out across the dark green canal, now flecked with pink and gold from the setting sun. 'It took me years to even come close to forming a theory on that one. It's partly because he's so absorbed in his work, and it's got worse the older he gets. There are only so many weeks and hours left to educate the world about the unique habitats the human race is ripping through, the species we're forcing into extinction. How can one "flighty" child compete against all of that?'

'What's the other part?'

Ruby looked up at him. 'He has plenty of friends and colleagues who have wild children—celebrity offspring syndrome, I've heard him call it. Overindulged, privileged, reckless. I think he wanted to save me from that.'

That was understandable, but surely anyone who knew Ruby knew she wasn't that sort. She might be impulsive, but that came from her creativity, not out of selfishness or arrogant stupidity.

She sighed and stood up, walked to the back of the boat, even though it was only a few steps. 'I came to understand his logic eventually. I think he thinks that if he rations out the attention and approval then he won't spoil me.' She sighed again. 'It's so sad, especially as I know he wasn't like that with my mother. He'd have given her anything.'

Max didn't say anything, mainly because he was rubbish at saying the right thing at the right time, but he also suspected she just needed room to talk.

'I can't live on the scraps he hands out,' she said sadly. 'He doesn't understand it, but women, be they wives or daughters or sisters, need more than that.'

They both fell into silence. Max thought of his mother, and wondered if Ruby was thinking of her too. He'd never wanted for approval from his father—not that the old man had ever said anything out loud—but they'd been so alike. It had been easy to see the things beneath the surface, hear the words his father had never been able to say. For the first time ever it struck him that maybe not everyone had that ability.

They'd been so different, Geoffrey and Serafina Martin. His mother emotional and demonstrative, his father stoic and silent. He'd always thought their extreme personality types should make them the perfect complement for each other, but maybe he'd been wrong. Maybe that had been the reason for his mother's midnight tears; she'd desperately needed to reap some of the tangible demonstrations of love she'd so generously sowed.

He nodded slowly. 'I'm starting to understand that.' He caught her eye. 'And it makes sense why it's easier to run away, rather than stay.'

He didn't like to say that. It went against everything in him, but he couldn't ignore the sense in it.

Ruby read him like a book. She laughed a soft little dry laugh. 'And you think you don't?'

Max stood up, his brows bunching together. No, he didn't run. He was the one that was solid, stuck things out.

She walked towards him, until she was standing right in front of him. 'You can't be fully committed to something if you keep part of yourself back. It's cheating—a bit like this lagoon.' She stretched her arm out to encompass the water, including the tiniest glimpse of the open sea in the distance. 'It looks like the deep blue sea, smells like it, tastes like it, but when you try and jump all the way in you find out how shallow it is. Commitment is easy when it's only ankle deep.'

Max wanted to be angry with her. He wanted to tell her she was so very wrong, but he couldn't. Instead he exhaled long and hard and met Ruby's enquiring gaze. 'That makes us two very similar creatures, then.'

She stared back at him, more than a hint of defiance in her expression. 'Yes.'

On the surface he and Ruby were chalk and cheese. She was quirky and outspoken, where he was taciturn and strait-laced. She was emotional and effusive, where he...wasn't. But underneath? Well, that was a whole different story.

Her eyes softened a little, but the hard-hitting honesty in them remained. 'Okay, I admit it. I'm a coward when it comes to my family. And maybe I do flit from thing to thing because I'm nervous about committing to anything fully, but you have to face it, Max, despite all your fine words, the only thing you're truly committed to when it comes to your family is your prejudice and lack of forgiveness.'

He turned and started up the engine again. The canals—even this wide, spacious one—we're closing in on him, and the sun would slip below the horizon soon. He headed out of the end of the Grand Canal and into the lagoon, so they could see the painfully bright orange smudge settling behind the monastery on Isola di San Giorgio. Out here the salty wind soothed him. He felt as if he could breathe properly again.

Ruby hadn't said anything since they'd set off again. She'd just sat down on the bench and crossed her arms. He slowed the motor and checked on her. She didn't look happy. He had a feeling he'd have no trouble keeping her at arm's length now. He might as well dig himself in further.

'Have you forgiven *your* father?'

She chewed her lip for a while. 'I hadn't realised I needed to, but maybe I do.' She looked up and noticed the sunset for the first time. 'Oh,' she said, her face lighting up, and Max couldn't bear to tear his eyes from her and turn around.

After staring for a moment, her focus changed and he could tell she was now studying him instead. 'I'm not sure it'll change anything. He'll probably still treat me the same way, but with you and Fina... It could change everything.'

'Maybe,' he said. And then he turned to watch the sun descend into the blue-grey water. They didn't say anything as it went down, just watched in silence, the only sound the gentle waves of the lagoon slapping against the hull of the little painted boat, then he started up the engine again. 'Do you want to go round the island?'

A twinkle of mischief appeared in her eyes, totally blindsiding him. 'You know what I'd really like?'

He shook his head.

'We're always being so safe when Sofia is in the boat, puttering around, going slow down the canals. I'd like to go out onto the open water and build up some speed, see what this little vintage baby can do.'

Max set off again at a moderate speed, at least until they'd rounded the large island in front of them and faced the open lagoon. Out here there was only the occasional ferry, plenty of room to let off some steam, and he discovered he was yearning for it as much as she was.

'Ready?' he asked, and shoved the throttle forward before she had time to answer.

Ruby squealed and hung on to the woodwork in front of her as the bow of the little boat lifted, skimming through the moonlit waves, and the wind rushed through their hair. At first she was silent, her breath taken by the change in speed, but as he circled around and the boat tilted she began to laugh, then she let out a loud whoop.

Max found himself laughing too, which was insane, seeing as how serious he'd been feeling only minutes earlier. He kept the speed up, took a few unexpected turns, raced the waves out towards Lido Island and then back again until they were both windswept and breathless.

As they circled the Isola di San Giorgio again, he reluctantly slowed the engine. The sky was a velvety midnight blue above them and the lights and reflections of Venice were threatening to outnumber the stars in their brilliance and beauty.

Ruby sighed. 'Can we stop here for a moment, before we head back home? I won't get a chance to see this again.'

He didn't answer, just circled one last time then flipped the key in the ignition and cut the engine. Ruby got up and walked shakily towards him as they got caught up in their own wake. She stopped before she got too close, though. Still out of reach. Just.

Another surge hit them. Max hardly noticed it, being used to boats as he was, but Ruby lost her footing, wobbled slightly.

Her arms, which had still been loosely hugged round herself, flew out for balance. At the same time he reacted on reflex and his hand shot out and curled round her elbow, steadying her.

Not at arm's length now. Not at all.

He looked down at where they were joined and wondered how hard it would be to let go. He looked up again to find Ruby's eyes large, but her expression calm and open. Very hard, he decided. Even after the boat had rocked itself back into equilibrium he found he hadn't been able to do it.

But maybe he didn't need to.

He slipped his hand down her arm, over her wrist, until his fingers met hers, and he laced them together, reminding himself of those intersecting arches he'd stolen for his design. How simple the shapes were on their own, but how much better they were when they were joined with something similar.

He reached for her other hand, meshed it to his in the same way. She looked down at their intertwined fingers, so tangled up with each other that he couldn't tell whether he was holding her or she was holding him, and then she looked back up at him, her breathing shallow, her cheeks flushed.

This was *way* more than ankle deep.

Gently he tugged, and she came. Their hands remained joined, and he bent his head to brush his lips against hers. It wasn't enough. He kissed her again, lingering this time. Ruby sighed and leaned against him. Gently she slid her fingers from his and ran her hands up his arms, onto his neck. He could feel her fingertips on the bare skin above his collar, her thumbs along his jaw.

She pulled away and opened her eyes. He looked back at her. Her fingers continued to roam, exploring his jaw and temple, tracing his cheekbones, and then they kissed again, sinking into it.

It wasn't like their first meeting of lips. It wasn't hot and urgent, fuelled by simple physical need, but neither was it hesitant and testing. It was slow and intimate, as if they'd been lovers for years, nothing but truth flowing between them, even if he was a little fuzzy on what exactly that truth was.

As the bells of the far away *campanili* rang out across the lagoon, and Venice glittered like a jewel in the distance, Max wrapped his arms around Ruby, pulled her as close as he could get. He might be rubbish with words, but he spoke to her in the poetry every Italian knew so well.

CHAPTER TWELVE

THEY DIDN'T GET BACK to the palazzo until well after nine. Max cut the engine and stared at the hulking exterior of his mother's house. Here, his and Ruby's roles were defined for them, clearly marked out. Out there on the lagoon, there had been nothing but a delicious blurring of all the reasons they shouldn't be together.

Ruby jumped out of the boat, took the rope from him and secured it to a post. Max stayed where he was in the boat.

He didn't want to go back inside.

For the last hour he'd felt alive again, free. The grief that had been the wallpaper of his life since his father's death had evaporated briefly, but now it was back again, slamming into his chest with such force he had to draw in a breath.

Ruby smiled at him, a sweet, beguiling smile, but he found he couldn't return it. Shutters were clanging up fast inside him, like those in a bank when the panic button had been pressed, and by the time he climbed out of the boat and headed inside no chink remained.

Each step up the staircase made him feel heavier, as if gravity were increasing.

'Max?' Ruby said as they reached the top, her eyes clouded with worry. He wanted to tell her it wasn't anything to do with her, that she was the only bright spot in his life at the moment, but the words didn't even make it up his throat, let alone out of his mouth.

He did what he could: he reached for her hand, caught it in his and wove his fingers into hers the way he'd done back on the boat just before he'd kissed her.

He saw relief flood her features and the smile came back. Sweeter this time, softer. What he wouldn't give to just lose himself in that smile.

'You have returned?' His mother's voice came from inside the salon.

Ruby jumped and slid her fingers from his before his mother appeared in the doorway. His skin felt cold where hers had just been.

'Why don't you come and have a coffee with me and tell me all about it?'

His mother looked hopefully at him, and Ruby joined her.

His head started to swirl—with the memories that had assaulted him earlier, with the conversation he'd had with Ruby out on the lagoon. He knew he should try with his mother, knew he should at least let her share her side of the story, that going in for coffee now would be a tiny and harmless step in that direction, but he couldn't seem to make his feet move.

'Max?' Ruby said, her smile disappearing, her brow creasing.

He felt as if he were made of concrete. 'I'm sorry,' he said, his voice a little hoarse, 'but I need to make up the time I took away from my work.'

Ruby's face fell. His mother just stared at him.

'I'm sorry,' he said again, and strode off in the direction of the library.

Ruby and Fina watched Max go. When the library door had shut behind him, Fina sighed and turned back into the salon.

'I don't blame him, you know,' she said as she walked to the coffee table and poured espresso into delicate cups. 'When things were at their worst between me and Geoffrey, I didn't behave well. He probably has many memories that make it easy for him to hate me.'

Ruby wanted to reach out to her, put a hand on her arm. 'I'm sure that's not true,' she said softly.

Fina shook her head. 'I loved that man, even though he was just as pig-headed as his son.' Fina sighed. 'I could have handled that. It was the fact he locked himself away…here.' She thumped her chest with her palm then looked Ruby right in the eye. 'I grew tired of hungering for something I thought he wouldn't—or couldn't—give me.'

Fina didn't pick up her coffee cup, but walked over to the windows and stared out. Ruby couldn't tell if she was focusing on the moon beyond or her reflection in the glass.

'I had glimpses of the man underneath,' she said. 'Foolishly, I thought that once we were married the process of slowly unravelling all that bound him would start. I tugged, pulled at threads, but I could never find the right place to begin.'

Ruby swallowed. She knew all about glimpses. Knew all about how tantalising they could be.

'In the end I used to do anything I could to provoke emotion from him. Anger was the easiest. I told myself that if I could make him feel *something* it proved he still cared.' She shook her head and looked at Ruby. 'I pushed him and pushed him. Doing things, saying things, I shouldn't have.

And each time I had to try harder, do more. I must have seemed like a monster to my son, but really I was just...' She paused, struggling for the right word.

'Desperate?' Ruby finished for her.

Fina gave her a grateful look. 'Yes.' She looked back at her reflection in the window. 'And in the end I succeeded. I pushed him to the ultimate limit.'

Ruby held her breath for a moment. 'What did you do?'

Fina blinked. 'I left him.'

Ruby stepped closer.

'It broke him,' Fina continued, her tone taking on a ragged quality. 'I finally had my proof. But I could never go back. I'd done too much damage.'

Ruby didn't know what to say, which was just as well, because if she'd tried to speak, tears would have coursed down her face. She just nodded, letting Fina know she was listening.

'It's my fault Massimo is the way he is,' Fina added softly, 'so I cannot be angry with him. I just don't want him to harden himself further, end up like his father.' She paused a moment and heaved in a breath. Ruby sensed she was trying not to lose composure completely. 'I shouldn't have left him behind, but I thought I was doing the right thing. He had his school…and Geoffrey adored him. I couldn't rob him of his son, too.'

'Of course you couldn't,' Ruby said.

Fina suddenly turned to face her, grabbed her hands and leaned in. 'Be careful when you fall in love,' she said hoarsely. 'It is a curse to love something so much, believe it is in easy reach, and then discover it will always be kept beneath lock and key.' Fina sighed dramatically and dropped her hands.

Ruby nodded and then stepped away, walked back to the table and picked up her espresso. She finished it quickly, even though it felt like gravel going down.

'I'd better check on Sofia,' she mumbled, then fled from the room.

Fina knew. Ruby didn't know how. Maybe she'd worked out that Ruby's dishevelled appearance after the boat ride had been down to more than a brisk twilight wind, but she knew. And she was warning Ruby off.

The morning was clear and bright. A light mist hovered over the lagoon and the Damiani family boat carved through it at speed as it headed away from the city and out into the open water. Max stood at the wheel, breeze lifting his hair, and concentrated on pinpointing their location. It had been a long time since he'd visited this place and he knew if he didn't pay attention that he'd miss it altogether.

'Where go?' Sofia piped up from the back of the boat.

He glanced over his shoulder and gave her a smile. Sofia was snuggled up between Ruby and his mother and all three of them were surrounded by a jumble of beach equipment—an umbrella, a picnic basket, various bags containing sunscreen and towels and changes of clothes.

He deliberately didn't catch Ruby's eye. Mainly because he was only just hanging on to the last bit of his control. The urge to touch her every time he saw her was quickly becoming overpowering— and had led to a few interesting stolen moments over the few days since their sunset trip. She was like a drug. The more he had, the more he wanted. Needed.

He took a deep breath and forced himself to behave. His mother and his not quite three-year-old niece were also in the boat; that should help somewhat. And it did. Just about.

'We're going to the beach,' he told Sofia and turned back round to concentrate on where he was going. A few moments later he slowed the motor and peered around, first at the water directly in front of the boat and then at the horizon, checking the location of various landmarks on the coast.

This was it. He was sure it was. He cut the motor and let down the small anchor.

'Want beach,' Sofia said, most determinedly, and Max threw her another smile.

'We're here.'

Ruby frowned at him. 'Don't tease her. She doesn't understand.'

'I'm not teasing,' he said. She was even adorable when she was cross with him, which was just as well, really, seeing as he was rather good at getting her in that state. He turned his attention to Sofia.

'This is a magic beach. You just wait and see.' And he stuck his thumb and forefinger in his mouth and whistled loudly. 'That's what gets the magic started,' he explained.

His mother just patted the child's hand and looked back at him with soulful eyes. This place had always been special to him, a highlight of their family holidays each year, and he knew she was experiencing the same rush of memories that he was. He'd thought it would help, bring them a sense of connection, but he managed to return her gaze for a second or so before he looked away.

He didn't have many memories of his father in Venice, especially as he'd often worked through the long summer holidays and had only joined them for snatched days and weekends, but this had been one of his favourite places. He'd been charmed by the sheer contrariness of it.

The tide had caused the boat to swing on its anchor slightly, just as he'd planned, and now he gave Sofia a salute, kicked off his shoes and jumped overboard.

'No!' screamed Ruby and stood up, but then she sat back down again with a plop when she realised he was standing and the water was only lapping round his calves. Sofia ran over to the edge of the boat and peered over the edge.

Ruby gave him an exasperated look and mouthed an insult that wasn't fit for Sofia's ears. He grinned back at her. Some primal part of him was stupidly pleased she'd been worried for him. She shook her head and smiled, rolling her eyes.

He didn't want to move, didn't want to do anything but stand here, the water turning his toes pruney, and look at her. It was the kind of thing he'd mocked his friends for doing when they'd met someone special, and had never, ever expected to fall prey to himself. He had to force himself to look away.

'Told you it was magic,' he said, and lifted Sofia out of the boat, lifejacket and all, and put her down beside him, careful to keep a grip on her hand. Sofia squealed, at first from the surprise of the cold water, but then from delight. He walked along a short length of the hidden sandbank just under the water then back to the boat.

'It's all very well having a magic beach,' Ruby said, trying to maintain an air of superiority and failing, 'but what good is it if it stays underwater?'

'You just wait and see. Coming in?'

Ruby nodded, and began stripping off her skirt to reveal shapely legs and the bottom half of her swimming costume. His mouth dried. He turned to his mother and raised an eyebrow.

'Don't be an idiot, Massimo. I'm far too old to be wading about in the lagoon. You just carry on and I'll enjoy the sun in the boat for a while.'

He nodded and held out his hand to Ruby so she could steady herself getting out of the boat. Once she was in the shallow water, they placed themselves either side of Sofia and went exploring. The remains of what once might have been an island was tiny, maybe only thirty metres by ten, but as they splashed around in the shallows, swinging Sofia between them, the tide crept away and revealed a perfect golden sandbank.

Sofia stood on the damp sand and stared at the grains beneath her feet. 'Magic,' she whispered. 'How do, Unc Max?'

He crouched down beside her. 'I whistled and it came.'

Sofia jammed all five fingers of her left hand in her mouth and puffed. 'No work,' she said, after she'd pulled them out again.

'That's because learning to whistle takes practice,' he told her. 'You have to do it again and again until you're good at it. When you're older, you'll be able to call the island, too. Everyone in our family can.' In the meantime, he showed her the basics—how to pucker her lips, how to blow gently. Sofia didn't manage to produce more than a raspy sound, but she seemed quite happy trying.

He looked up at Ruby. 'Can you whistle?'

She smiled and rolled her eyes. 'Not like you. In comparison my efforts seem pathetic.'

Max stood up, still holding Sofia's hand. The

patch of sand was growing now, the almost imper-
ceptible tilt of the land helping the tide to recede
rapidly. 'Let's all whistle together, and perhaps
the rest of the island will come.'

So they stood solemnly in a row, faced the
lagoon, and blew, his whistle loud and long,
Ruby's slightly throaty, with a unique little trill
at the end, and Sofia's determined puffing filling
out their little orchestra.

It was strange. He'd found it hard to be at the
island again at first, but bringing Ruby here was
changing that. Somehow she soothed the dark
voices in his head away, made him believe he
could be free of them one day.

When they'd finished they headed back to the
boat and began unloading their beach stuff. He
set up the umbrella and spread the blanket while
Ruby held on to Sofia. Fina directed from the
bow of the boat, and only when it was all set up
to her liking did she consent to let him pull the
boat closer so she could step onto dry sand.

They ate their lunch under the umbrella, a simple affair of meats and cheeses, bread and olives,
and when they'd finished Ruby grabbed a towel,
headed out from under the shade of the umbrella
and laid it on the sand. She unbuttoned her white,

Fifties-style blouse and shrugged it off, to reveal a matching swimsuit.

Not matching in colour, because it was a deep ruby red with large black roses all over it, but matching in style. It was one of those weird things he'd seen in old-fashion photos, with a wide halter-neck strap, a ruched front and a leg line that was low, completely covering her bottom and reaching to the tops of her thighs. It should have been unflattering, and on many women it would have looked like a Halloween costume, but on Ruby it looked sensational. She reminded him of those sirens with the rosy cheeks, red lips and long legs that he'd seen painted on the side of wartime planes.

'I didn't think you'd remember the whistle,' his mother muttered beside him, her eyes a little misty.

His first reaction was to bristle, to bat the comment away and pretend he hadn't heard it. Of course he'd remembered. It had been his father's trick to call the island that way. For a man who'd had a hard time expressing his emotions, he'd been unusually imaginative. It had made him a good architect, but it had made him an even better father, softening the gruff edges.

He turned and watched Ruby as she finished getting her towel just so, then lay down on top of it to face the sun.

He thought about her willingness to try and try again, even when things didn't go according to plan. She never gave up, never locked herself away from new experiences. Never locked herself away from hope that it would all turn out right one day. She wasn't weak and flaky, as he'd thought her. She was strong. Resilient.

And she was right. He needed to try with his mother. Not just for the sake of his family, but because he wanted to be the kind of man who was worthy of Ruby Lange. The kind of man who knew how to do more than just 'ankle deep'. That was what she needed, and that was what he wanted to give her.

His mother was staring out to sea, and had obviously given up on him giving her an answer. For the first time he saw it—what Ruby had been trying to tell him about—the deep pain behind her eyes. The same kind of desolation he'd seen his father wear in unguarded moments, the same one that had eaten away at him, until it had sucked the life right out of him.

Something warm flooded his chest. Something

that wasn't bitterness or rage or judgement, something that made him remember how warm and kind she'd been when he'd been younger, how she'd have given anything for her children, and even more for her husband.

Words rushed around inside his head, the beginnings of sentences. The beginnings of a truce.

But none of them left his mouth. It felt as if he were looking at his mother from behind a large sheet of bulletproof glass. There was so much he wanted to say, so many questions he wanted to ask, but he found he could release none of them. It wouldn't come, even though, for the first time in almost two decades, he wanted it to. He wanted to *try*.

Eventually his mother picked up a book and began to read. Max sat there, adrenaline making his blood surge and his skin prickle, but anyone looking at him would have thought he was resting his hands on his knees, relaxing in the sun. He twisted his head and searched for a flowery red and black costume.

For most of his life he'd been proud when people had called him his father's son, when they'd remarked on the likeness, not just in looks but in temperament, but for the first time that pride chilled into fear. If he was the cookie-cutter off-spring everyone always said he was, there was a real chance that he would never deserve a woman like Ruby Lange.

CHAPTER THIRTEEN

RUBY RETURNED TO THE SALON that evening after dinner to tidy some of Sofia's things away. She sorted through a stack of drawing papers, thinking she'd find one or two to present to Fina as a memento of Sofia's visit.

She reached a shortlist of seven. Some drawings that she'd done and Sofia had coloured in, and a few of her charge's own creations. They needed skilful interpretation, but the intent was there. Ruby stopped as she stared at a page that was filled with different-coloured crayon blobs, all lined up. The shocking pink blob was Fina, apparently. The smaller one next to her, a vibrant, bright yellow, was Sofia herself. The dark blue one off to the side, looking a bit like a navy, vertical thundercloud, was Max. Ruby had giggled at that when Sofia had pointed it out.

That only left the purple blob.

The purple blob so close to the blue one they

practically merged at the edges, creating an in-
digo smudge.

It was understandable, Ruby supposed, that
Sofia should put her and Max next to each other.
She spent a lot of time with the pair of them, after
all. Ruby had smiled when Sofia had told her the
scribble of purple was her, honoured to have been
included, but now she looked at it she realised just
how much artistic licence Sofia had taken.

But Max didn't do that, did he? He didn't let his
edges blur like that. And maybe he never would.

That was what Fina had been trying to tell her.

Was she just fooling herself?

Ruby sighed and sank onto the rug. The pieces
of paper she'd collected fluttered out of her hand
and fell onto the floor unseen. She was so confused.

They'd spent a lot of time together over the last
five days. Not just the morning outings with Sofia,
but in the evenings Fina often disappeared to visit
her friend Renata after they'd eaten dinner, then
Ruby would creep into the library and she'd have
a glorious hour or two alone with Max.

When she was with him, everything was amazing and she couldn't think about anything else.
When he kissed her, she felt as if she were touch-

ing something deep inside him. More and more he was giving her 'glimpses' of the real Max, and each time she dived deeper in she got lost a little more. One day soon there'd be no going back.

But then she'd leave him and the little doubts would start to creep in, nibbling away at her.

He had to feel the same way, didn't he? The truth of it rang between them every time they were in the same room together, and she really wanted to believe it, but...

Never once had he mentioned where this was going—or even *if* it was going—once their stay in Venice ended. Never once had he put words to how he felt about her, given her any hint about the future. Their days here were numbered; she knew that. Gia had phoned saying she needed a little longer in L.A., but the original fortnight was up in just two days' time.

She sighed and collected the pieces of paper together and put them away in the sideboard with the other drawing things, forgetting that she'd sorted out the masterpieces and jumbling them back in with the others again.

Once she was finished putting them away she headed for the library. Max was poring over his laptop, as usual, but when he saw her he got up from his chair and crossed the room to where she was standing just near the doorway. He stood close, far too close for a boss approaching his employee, then gave her an impish smile as he closed the door behind her, pressed her up against it and kissed her until her head was spinning and her lungs were convinced oxygen was just a deep and distant memory.

When he pulled back to look at her, she saw a flash of something in his eyes. Something deep. Something true. It sent her heart spinning like the waltzer at the fairground. She so wanted to forget about tomorrow and just do what felt right for now, but that was how she'd spent her whole life so far, and it was time to step back and take a more mature approach. Where Max was concerned, she really needed to pay attention to the big picture.

She wanted him to say something.

Exactly what, she didn't know. Just something. Something that she didn't have to prise out of him. Something to let her know what was happening between them, if he was as confused as she was, but Max just leaned in and stole another kiss. It made her blood dance right down to her toes.

She pulled away, looked him in the eyes. 'What are we doing?' she whispered.

Just one of Max's eyebrows hitched up a little. 'I thought we'd covered enough ground for you to be sure, but if you want a little more demonstration?'

He leaned close again, but Ruby stopped him with her hands on his chest. Hands that dearly craved a little more 'demonstration', but she forced them to stay put instead of using them to explore him further.

'I mean *us*. Is this just a holiday fling, or what?'

He frowned. She'd upset him, she could tell, but she had to know. She'd spent her whole life straining for the crumbs one man doled out to her. She'd had no choice but to accept what her father gave her, but with Max she did, and she'd be insane to follow that pattern with him. *Glimpses* were all well and good for now, but for the long term? That was like trying to nourish yourself with only a diet of canapés for the rest of your life.

'Ruby? Don't you know?'

She shook her head. All she knew was that she had a choice: dive in and hope that one day Max would shed the same chains that had bound his father, or run now before things got even more serious.

More serious? Hah. She was kidding herself. She was already half in love with him. It wouldn't take much more to push her over the precipice.

Max's hands moved to circle her waist, to pull her as close as she could possibly get without their physical boundaries blurring just as they had done in Sofia's drawing. *'Lascia che ti mostri.'*

Let me show you.

When he touched her lips with his again she just about melted clean away. She'd thought she'd experienced passion from Max before. She now realised they'd just been paddling in the shallows. But even as he unleashed the force of it on her, as the kiss continued, she got the sense that Max was a like a dam, holding back the pressure of a million gallons of water. There was still more beneath, so much more.

She wanted him to tear that last barrier down, to unleash the torrent and let it sweep her away, but the structure was solid, impenetrable. Nothing she could do could get it to crack. A tiny part of her cried out in pain as she realised that, even in this, Max was holding himself back.

He picked her up and carried her to the small love seat in the corner of the room, and they both fell onto it in a tangle of arms and legs, hot breath and pounding hearts, and as his lips found the curve of her neck and his hands smoothed down her body she discovered something did crumble after all. But it was all her good resolves, not him.

Ruby lay in bed that evening and reached for her mobile phone, which had lain untouched most of the last fortnight. Partly because it was too expensive to turn data roaming on, but also because she was avoiding communication from her father about The Job.

However, she'd started fantasising about carrying on back in London with Max, about being the kind of woman he'd consider sharing his life with. That clearly meant that the world was upside down and back-to-front, and she obviously needed a sharp dose of reality to counteract that and help her think straight. And a *What have you done now?* lecture and an exorbitant phone bill would do nicely on that front.

Just as she feared, an email from dear old dad was lurking in her inbox. She shifted position, took a deep breath and opened it.

FAO: Ruby Lange.

That was typical Dad. Other people started emails with *Hi!* or *Hey!* or just launched into the subject at hand as quickly as possible. Only Patrick Lange could make an informal communication sound like a court summons.

Dear Ruby,
I had hoped to hear from you by now on your current employment situation. I understand from your flatmate that you are in Europe somewhere, doing something, but she could not enlighten me any further. Would you care to? I'm holding the job open for you, and I'd greatly appreciate it if you could let me know if you're going to take it. There are plenty of other people who would kill for this kind of opportunity, you know.

Yes, she knew. He'd told her often enough.

You need to approach life with a more adult attitude, Ruby. You can't flit around for ever 'finding yourself'. At your age it's time you stopped running away from responsibility and started embracing it.
I need to know about the production assistant

position before next Monday. Please get in contact and let me know.
Dad x

Ruby scowled at her mobile screen. No *I know
I've been incommunicado for a month, but how
are you doing, Ruby?* No *Great you've found
yourself a new job, Ruby!* Just judgement and how
much she was disappointing him, as always.

She knew she really shouldn't message angry,
but she couldn't help herself.

Thanks for the vote of confidence, Dad.

Much to her surprise, her message alert went
off a few minutes later.

Ruby, understand that I don't say the things I do
to hurt you. You have so much potential and it's a
crime to waste it drifting from thing to thing. The
job offer stands. I think you might enjoy it, and I
expect you will be good at it. You have just the
right kind of energy the team needs. D x

Ruby flipped her phone case closed and put her
mobile back on the bedside table. She didn't know

whether to be angry that she'd finally forced him into giving her a backhanded compliment or just stupidly happy he thought she could be good at something. She folded her arms across her chest on top of the quilt and stared at the ceiling.

Well, she'd wanted reality, and her father had dished up some five-star fare.

But there was a difference between not being able to stick with something and not wanting to. Why didn't he understand that?

Because it looks the same, smells the same, tastes the same...

No. It wasn't the same. It was always her choice. Always her decision.

You choose to get that itchy feeling, want to feel it torment you until you have no other option but to outrun it?

She scowled at the pretty looping baroque designs on the ceiling. Now even her subconscious was ganging up on her. That wasn't true, was it? That feeling of being pinned down, of getting so close to something to feel its heat, to feel how much it could scorch and burn, that wasn't what made her seek out new and exciting things. It couldn't be.

But as she followed the patterns and shapes

on the ceiling with her eyes she catalogued all the jobs she'd had over the last five years, all the people and places she'd thought she'd become attached to, and she discovered there wasn't one time that she hadn't left because, not only had her feet got itchy, but her whole being had got itchy. She used to think it was the yearning for fresh pastures that made her feel that way, but now she was staring it in the face, dissecting it and pulling it apart, she saw it for what it really was.

Fear.

Plain and simple.

You're not a free spirit, Ruby Lange. You're a coward.

There wasn't one time she hadn't succumbed to that itch, except...

Except that night almost a week ago on the dock, when it had been itching so hard she'd almost jumped into the canal to stop the burning. When Max had asked her to stay. And she had.

Ruby let out a long and shuddering breath.

She wanted to stick with Max. No matter what. She wanted that with all her heart.

The realisation shocked her. It should have made her heart race and her breathing shallow, but all she felt instead of blind panic was a strange but not unwelcome sense of peace creeping up on her.

Ruby threw the covers back, jumped out of bed and walked over to stare out of the window. For some reason, the gently lapping water soothed her, helped her think.

She had to be sure about this.

Not just about Max's feelings for her, but about her feelings for Max. If they went forward with this, and he held back from her, she knew she wouldn't be able to stay around and let her heart endlessly beg for more. Look at what that had done for Fina.

But she also knew that if she dived into this relationship, and then bailed, it might seal his fate. He would shut down completely. And that would lead to consequences, not just for her, but possibly for Fina and Sofia and the rest of his family. Max had so much to give, if he would only let himself, and she didn't want to be the reason he didn't.

She started to pace. Back and forth, back and forth she went. She finally fell into bed and tossed back and forth there too. At 3:00 a.m. she punched her pillow hard and let out a low moan of frustration.

The only thing solid she could come up with

was that she'd rather be with Max than without him. And she could do it, she knew she could, but it was one thing for her to be sure of it, and another entirely to convince Max of the same.

Another realisation hit her straight between the eyebrows. Maybe that was why he was holding back! Maybe it was nothing to do with him and everything to do with her.

She wouldn't blame him if he didn't trust her not to run when things got sticky. Her track record was all hundred-metre dashes: exciting and adrenaline-inducing while they lasted, but over quickly and leaving everyone feeling burnt out and exhausted. She needed to convince him she was capable of a marathon; that she'd changed in the space of two short weeks and was ready to do more. Be more. That she was a safe pair of hands for his heart.

But how?

Words wouldn't be enough. Max was all about the concrete, the tangible evidence. She'd have to prove it to him in no uncertain terms. She went back to staring at the ceiling, familiar with its intricate patterns and leafy trails now, and after only a few moments the solution dropped into her brain with a thud.

Of course! It was perfect.

She rolled over, picked up her phone and began typing in an email with her thumbs.

CHAPTER FOURTEEN

THE PLANS FOR the institute were almost finished. It was just as well, because, although he had got up at four the last few days to put in the hours needed, the whole time he worked away at his desk there was an internal timer that clicked away within him, counting down the seconds to ten o'clock, when he could rise from his desk, shove the papers away and go and see her.

Every day was a surprise, something new. And he didn't just mean her wardrobe, although it was an endless source of fascination to him that the handful of clothes she'd stuffed into that rucksack could be combined in so many different ways to create so many different looks.

No, he meant Ruby. Every day she brought him something fresh, something exciting. When he'd first met her, he'd thought she needed to grow up and settle down, but now he realised how fearless, how magnificent she was. He didn't want her to change a thing about herself.

The timer on his watch beeped at him and he looked up from his desk. Two minutes to ten. It was time. He'd done his duty, done his hours, and now he could spend time with Ruby. He didn't even mind that Sofia was always thrown into the mix.

To be honest, he was glad to have a reason to take things slowly. Otherwise he wasn't sure he'd be able to help himself. She wanted new experiences? She wanted romance? He wanted to show her just how amazing Venice could be, just how it could imprint itself on a soul. He wanted to talk about dreams and plans and for ever. And he would have done, if not for one thing: he didn't want to scare her off. It was only a supreme act of will that prevented him spilling it all out to her and laying it at her feet.

Breathe, Max. Give the girl time. Don't spook her.

He just needed to get the groundwork in before Gia arrived back to claim Sofia.

He slowed in the corridor that led to the salon, took a moment to inhale and exhale, and then he turned the corner and walked through the door.

As he often found them when he arrived for his morning session with his niece, she and Ruby were drawing. Sofia was colouring-in a princess in a flowing robe, having got over her 'naughty fish' obsession, and Ruby was bent over her sketch-book. He crept up behind her while she was absorbed and sneaked a look.

She was working on a drawing of a gondola floating in front of a palazzo. Her style was interesting. She often drew in black pen, but the lines were always fluid and emotive. It should have given a messy look to the sketch, but somehow she managed to get the shape and structures perfectly without making it look staid and formal, something he could never have done. And he could see she was growing, developing. There was a new confidence in her work that hadn't been there when she'd arrived.

That was the elusive 'niche' she'd been looking for, he was sure of it, but he sensed she lacked confidence to pursue it. He wondered what he could do to encourage her. She'd helped him rediscover the real excitement and passion that had been missing from his work for months now, and he'd like to return the favour.

She started, suddenly realising he was close, jumped up and turned round, smiling. 'Nosey,' she said.

The air crackled between them, and he bent down and stole a kiss. 'Guilty as charged.' He nodded at his niece, who'd almost finished obliterating her princess in a cloud of bright orange crayon so thick one could hardly see the black lines of Ruby's pen underneath.

Ruby chuckled. 'She's nothing if not thorough. I have no idea where she gets that from.'

'Shut up,' he said. 'Are you ready to go?'

She nodded. 'We're off to feed the pigeons in St Mark's Square, right?'

He didn't answer. When he'd mentioned pigeons, it wasn't necessarily feeding them he'd been thinking about, seeing as the city was trying to actively discourage it. Chasing them had been a much preferred boyhood pastime, one he thought Sofia would enjoy with equal relish, and almost verged on the side of civic duty these days, as the birds caused so much damage to the delicate buildings and statues.

When Ruby stood back, he frowned. Something was different. Something was not quite right....

And then he realised what it was. He'd seen that outfit before. It was the plain T-shirt and jeans she'd worn a couple of times before, but today it was unadorned. No loops of beaded necklaces, no vintage waistcoat, no floaty scarves. It was most odd. But since Ruby had always been one to defy expectation where her wardrobe was concerned, he supposed she was following true to form.

It should have only taken ten minutes to walk to St Mark's from Ca' Damiani, but it took Max, Ruby and Sofia closer to twenty. Mostly because they didn't bother with the buggy and had to accommodate Sofia's tiny little legs. When they were there, Sofia delighted in chasing the pigeons, which flew up in clouds as she cut a path through them, but settled back down nearby only seconds later.

He and Ruby watched on from the sidelines, smiling. He reached over and took her hand, relished the feel of her warm skin in his. She always felt that way, never cold, always soft and inviting.

'That drawing you were doing this morning was very good,' he told her. 'I really think you should do something with it.' He thought about the overpriced prints and postcards for the tourists, the sickly, sentimental paintings in some of the shops that sold carnival masks by the bucketload. 'Your drawings of Venice are better than a lot of what's out there.'

He thought she'd be pleased at some encouraging words, but she pressed her lips together and stared out across the vast square with its arcades and hundreds of pillars. 'Nah,' she said, lifting just one shoulder in a little shrug. 'I think it's better if I keep it as a hobby for now.'

His brows drew together as he waited for her to carry on, say something more cheery and upbeat, but she just let out a huge sigh. Something really was different, and it wasn't just the wardrobe.

'Come on,' he said, 'let's walk a bit more.'

She nodded and called for Sofia, who wasn't that enthralled at the idea of leaving the pigeons alone, but she came without too much grizzling.

It wasn't just today, was it? This strange behaviour. There had been little things for the past few days. Tiny things he'd hardly noticed when they'd been random, individual occurrences, but now they were building to make something bigger, forming themselves into a pattern. She'd been quieter, more restrained. She'd laughed less. And there was something else, too, about the way she looked that was different. Something other than the lack of accessories. He just couldn't put his finger on what it was.

Was this connected to the drawing thing?

She talked about passion, about wanting to

find it. It was clear to him that drawing was what she really loved to do. She couldn't *not* do it. He couldn't count the number of scraps of paper, backs of receipts, paper napkins he'd seen her sketches on in the last couple of weeks. So why did she resist it? Why did she avoid it when the thing that tugged her heart most was under her nose?

They walked out towards the Doge's Palace. He'd been going to tell her some interesting facts about it, things linked to conversations they'd had earlier in the week, but now it just felt like the wrong thing to do, so they strolled in silence to the water's edge and stared over to Isola di San Giorgio. Out on the lagoon, he could see the exact spot he'd cut the motor on their sunset trip, but there was no moonlight now, no gently flickering stars, just bright sun, beating down on them and bleaching all the shadows away.

'I've got something to tell you,' she said, after they'd been staring at the water for a couple of minutes. 'It's really great news.'

She twisted to look at him, but the smile she wore seemed hollow, like the trompe l'oeil in his mother's salon. It had the appearance of reality, but there was no depth to it.

'I've decided to take the job with my father's production company.' She looked at him, waiting for a response.

Max froze as the vague feeling that had plagued him all morning solidified into something hard and nasty, turning his insides cold. This wasn't her dream, her passion. In fact, it was the very opposite of what she'd said she'd wanted out of life.

He shook his head. 'Why?'

Her smile disappeared. '*Why?* Not "well done, Ruby. Good on you for choosing something you're going to stick to"?'

His mouth moved. He had *not* seen that coming. 'I thought it was the last thing you wanted.'

She shrugged and bent to retie Sofia's shoelace, which had come undone, then stood up again. 'I thought about what you said about finding the perfect thing by doing the hard stuff. Maybe you're right. And since my parents were both nuts about television and nature, maybe it's in my genes. Who knows?'

'Don't do it,' he said, and she turned to face him, shocked.

'Max, you are making no sense. I thought you'd be overjoyed at this. I thought you'd understand.'

He could tell she was hurt by the way she folded

her arms across her middle, by the way she rubbed the toe of her shoe against the flagstones.

'It's too late, anyway' she said quietly. 'I've already formally accepted the offer.'

'When?'

The toe ground harder into the floor. 'Two days ago.'

He wanted to grab hold of her, to tell her not to turn her back on her dreams, to run with them and to hell with the consequences. He wanted to tell her to try every damn job in the universe if she liked, not to care what anybody else said, as long as she didn't give up. This was worse. This was way worse than not finishing something. For some reason he sensed Ruby was waving the white flag of defeat.

He wanted to tell her all of that and more. That he loved her. That he wanted her to brighten his day every day for the rest of his life. But he didn't. Couldn't. What if he got too intense too soon and scared her away? He didn't think he could bear it.

He opened his mouth, got ready to say something. Anything. He had to tell her something of how he felt, even if he only let a fraction of it slip, but then he realised what he'd been trying to put his finger on, what else had changed about her. He closed his mouth again and stared.

As she looked at her feet the sun glinted off her dark hair. It looked beautiful, shiny and thick, but not one hint of purple remained.

Ruby knocked softly on the library door. It was ten past ten and Max hadn't turned up for their usual session with Sofia. The day was grey and drizzly, the mist hanging so low over the whole city that the tops of the buildings seemed to melt into the white sky. A castle-building session was much needed.

'Yes?' came his reply from behind the door.

Ruby hesitated for a second. He didn't sound angry exactly, but there was a definite edge to his voice. She pushed the door and leaned in, keeping her feet on the threshold. 'It's past ten.'

He didn't turn round for a moment, just kept making deft, straight lines on a piece of paper with a pencil. When he turned round a faint scowl marred his features. It was just the concentration of working on his plans, right? As far as she was aware she hadn't done anything wrong in the last few days. In fact, she was doing her level best to do everything right, to prove to Max that she could be the kind of woman he could rely on.

'I don't think I'm going to be able to join you today,' he said, his voice neutral.

'Oh.' It took Ruby a moment to adjust to that information. They'd got into such a rhythm that it felt as if they'd missed a step and everything had jarred. And then there was the fact that he hadn't taken the opportunity to grab her, press her up against the wall and kiss her until she was breathless, a ritual she'd come to look forward to.

'But you promised your mother—'

'I promised my mother I'd stick to her terms for a week. I did that—and more. My agreement with her has ended, Ruby.'

She frowned, then nodded. She hadn't thought about it that way, but she supposed he was right. He hadn't needed to come out with her and Sofia for the last week. It should have made her happy that he'd possibly done so in order to spend time with her, but the expression on his face stopped that. It was like glass. Hard, solid, reflecting everything back at her.

He also hadn't softened one iota with his mother. That scared her. And not just for Fina's sake. Were those walls of his ever going to come fully down?

'The deadline for getting the final plans into the National Institute of Fine Art is next week,' he explained calmly. 'I have to focus on that for a while.'

'Okay,' she said slowly. For some reason she felt she was missing something here. Something big. Or was she just being paranoid? 'We'll miss you.'

Max just nodded. His body shifted, and she could tell he was itching to get back to his plans. She did her best not to take it personally, not to take it as a rejection.

'Will we see you at dinner this evening?'

A bit of the familiar, world-weary Max she'd met at the beginning of their trip returned. 'My mother has insisted I take you out to eat. She told me in no uncertain terms that it's a travesty that you've spent more than a fortnight in a city full of fabulous restaurants and haven't sampled their food yet.'

'Oh,' Ruby said again. 'That's lovely.'

Maybe Fina had decided she'd been wrong about what she'd said to her. Ruby had grown more and more suspicious that Fina's evenings out visiting Renata had quickly become an excuse to give them time alone together. Maybe she thought there was hope for her and Max after all.

Then why wasn't Ruby happy about that? Why did her stomach feel as heavy as a bowling ball?

Max just gave her a single nod.

Silence filled the space between them.

'Well…I'll just go and…' Ruby gestured in the direction of the salon. 'I'll see you this evening.'

'This evening,' Max echoed, but he'd already turned and started making swift lines on his plans.

Ruby slid her body from the space between door and frame and closed it softly behind her.

CHAPTER FIFTEEN

WHEN IT WAS TIME to leave that evening, instead of jumping in the launch via the boat door Max lead Ruby out of Ca' Damiani's tiny, almost dowdy street entrance, through a little, high-walled court-yard and out of a nondescript wooden door. There, the narrow *calle* opened onto a wider one, and within five minutes they had entered a secluded little square with a few restaurants and shops that were closed for the night.

They headed for an unremarkable-looking res-taurant almost in the corner of the *campo*, with a dull, cappuccino-coloured awning and a few tables and chairs outside. The inside, however, was always a surprise after the mundane exterior. There were whitewashed brick walls and dark wood panelling. A counter stretched down one side, full of doors and drawers, reminiscent of an old-fashioned haberdashery shop. A gramophone perched on a table in the corner and glasses and bottles of wine filled what looked like a bookshelf at the far end of the space.

Ruby turned to him and grinned. He'd guessed she'd like this place. It was quirky and unique, as she was. And it didn't hurt that it served some of the best seafood in Venice.

They sat at a small table in the corner, overlooking the square, decked out in thick white linen and spotlessly shiny silverware.

It should have been romantic.

It was.

Well, it would have been, but for the conversation he knew had to come. One neither of them would like, but was totally, totally necessary. His plan to work on his designs that morning had been shot to pieces after Ruby's visit, and he'd spent the couple of hours until lunchtime mulling their situation over and over.

Ruby was changing herself. For him. He'd finally realised that when he'd noticed she'd dyed her hair. The clothes, the more sedate version of Ruby who'd appeared over the last couple of days…it all made sense now. And he hated himself for it.

He *needed* her to be the Ruby he'd fallen in love

with, couldn't settle for anything less. Drastic action was needed.

He wanted to tell her that over dinner, as they ate their marinated raw fish starters, but it was as if there were a glass wall between them. Not a thin sliver, either, that could have been shattered with a ball or a fist, but one ten inches thick that repelled his words, weighed him down.

Was this what his father had felt when he'd looked at his mother? Everything swirling inside so hard and so fast he thought it might consume him with no way to let it out? He feared it was.

Geoffrey Martin had loved his vibrant Italian wife so much. Max had always known that, always respected it. But now he saw that maybe his father had grasped too hard and given too little back. Serafina had been what he'd needed to bring him out of his shell, balance him out, but he hadn't been what she'd needed. Or had chosen not to be. For the first time in his life, Max realised his father had been selfish, and that had created an imbalance in the relationship that had ultimately doomed it to failure.

The same kind of imbalance he was aware of when he thought about himself and the petite, vibrant woman sitting opposite him, eating her blackened sea bass.

He would not make the same mistake. He would not be a coward and make Ruby pay for his weakness. He wouldn't let her crush her spirit for him, deny everything she was and wanted to be. It was too high a price to pay. But there was only one way he could think of preventing that, even if it meant a colourless, bleak future ahead for himself. But he'd do it—for her.

He took a deep breath, hoping she'd answer differently this time, hoping she'd spare them both. 'Are you still determined to take that job with your father?'

Ruby looked up from her fish and met Max's gaze. When he'd mentioned going out to dinner this evening, she'd thought the conversation might have been a little more…intimate. This was a wonderful chance for them to be away from the palazzo, to be romantic with each other, and yet he wanted to talk about her father? Talk about a passion killer.

'Yes.' She was determined to show him she could stick at something, think about the big picture rather than just the details of the here and now.

He sighed. 'I wish you wouldn't.'

She put her knife and fork down and looked at him helplessly. 'Why?'

'Because it's not your passion.'

She reached for her wine glass. 'It could be my passion. Like you said, how do I know if I don't try?'

To be honest, she didn't care about the job. It was just a means to an end. What she was really passionate about was being with Max. But in his current strange mood, she wasn't sure he was ready to hear that. She'd do anything it took. Anything. Even taking that job with her father.

'And I can't say anything to change your mind?'

She shook her head. 'No.' Max wanted to see if she could stick to something? Well, she wasn't budging on this, even if it killed her.

He went back to eating his food, his expression grim. What had she said now?

They finished their meals, only punctuating the silence with odd snatches of meaningless conversation, until their espressos came, then Max sat up straighter and looked her in the eye. 'I need to talk to you about something…something important.'

His expression was so serious, but instead of making her jittery, it melted her heart. He was so earnest, so full of wanting to do the right thing, and she loved him for it. When Max's heart was in something, it was all-in, and she could allow him a little severity in return for that. She reached out and covered his hand with hers across the table. His skin felt cool and smooth.

'I told you when I hired you that this was going to be a two-week job at most and we've exceeded that now.'

This was it. This was the conversation. About where they were going when they got back to London, her stupid secret fantasies on the verge of coming true. Ruby forced herself to sit still and listen, which was hard with her heart fluttering about madly inside her ribcage like a trapped bird. She nodded, encouraging him to keep going.

'Well, I think it's time your contract came to an end.'

Ruby blinked. That wasn't what she'd expected him to say at all. Was this a particularly 'Max' way of saying their relationship was moving fully from professional to personal? 'Okay. So when are we heading back to London?'

He swallowed. 'I'm not, but you are.'

Ruby removed her hand from on top of his and sat back. 'I don't understand.'

'I can't begin to thank you for the way you've helped me change,' he said, and while his expression remained granite-like his eyes warmed. She could feel her heart reaching out to him, even as all her other instincts told her to back away. 'But it's time for me to fly solo.'

'What does that mean?'

He broke eye contact. 'I need to learn to interact with my family without having you there as both catalyst and buffer. I need to learn to do it on my own, Ruby.'

She shook her head, not really sure which bit of information she was rejecting, or why. 'But I can just keep out of the way... I can...'

He shook his head. 'You've been amazing, but now it's time for you to go home.' A gruff laugh followed. 'I'd say it was time for you to travel, to explore, to find whatever it is you're looking for in life, but you're determined to take that damn job with your father.'

She frowned. 'Yes, I am. But what has that got to do with anything?'

He just looked at her, as if he was trying to send a message with his eyes, but she got nothing. Those walls were back up, weren't they? He was shutting her out. Her stomach dropped as she realised that was what this had all been about. He'd been pulling away slowly for the last couple of days, hadn't he? She'd just been too stupidly in love with him to notice.

You've finally done it, Ruby. Brava. You've jumped in with your heart, given it wholly and completely, and the man you've given it to doesn't want it. He's handing it back to you on a plate. Thanks, but no, thanks.

Part of her couldn't quite believe it.

'But when you get back to London, will we...?'

Now the message from his eyes got through. Loud and clear.

No.

There would be no London.

There would be no Max for her. All they would ever have was what had happened here in Venice.

'Max?' she croaked.

He shook his head. 'I'm sorry, Ruby. Professionally speaking, I don't need you any longer.'

She swallowed. 'And personally?'

Max didn't say anything, just sat ramrod straight in his chair, jaw tense, eyes empty.

That was when the bird inside stopped fluttering madly. In fact, Ruby wasn't sure there was any movement at all any more.

* * *

She'd never been fired from a job—mainly because she always left before that kind of eventuality arose—but Max had managed to make her first experience of it a real doozy.

I don't need you.

Professional and personal rejection in one go. Nice shot.

She got up, threw her napkin down and walked out of the restaurant.

Thankfully, the fact they'd walked here meant she could find her way back to the palazzo on her own, and once there she'd pack. In *three* minutes. And then she'd be out of here, and there was no way Max Martin would stop her this time.

He caught up with her not long afterwards, as she was leaving a wider street and turning into a narrow, cobbled one.

'Ruby!'

Heavy footsteps pounded behind her, getting closer. She kept walking.

'Where are you going?' He didn't sound flustered or bothered at all, just slightly out of breath from the running. It made her want to scream.

Home, she almost said, but then she realised just

how stupidly inaccurate that was. 'Back to the palazzo,' she said. 'I thought that was obvious.'

He fell into step beside her, and the narrowness of the *calle* meant he was far too close. 'You don't have to leave straight away. Wait until the morning.'

That sounded so generous, so reasonable. She regretted not having that contract now, because maybe, just maybe, she could have found something in it so she could sue his sorry hide for breaching it, for false advertising…*something*. There was no way she was staying here overnight. What did he want her to do? Lie in bed and cry over him? She wasn't that girl. It was time to move on. Onwards and upwards, remember?

She stomped down the street, glad she was wearing her ballet flats. They might not produce a satisfying echo, but they did make for a quick getaway. How could she have read him so wrong?

A series of images flashed through her head: kissing on the boat as the sun set over the lagoon, watching him building castles with Sofia the very first time, the moment that stupid little crab had bit her on the finger, and, last, the way he'd whistled for an island to appear out of the sea.

She stopped walking.

That was the real Max. She was sure of it.

He froze beside her, but she kept staring straight ahead.

She'd lived in the same house as this man for two weeks, and one thing she knew: he wasn't that good of a liar. He might keep things locked away, but he wasn't a man to kiss and run, to promise one thing with his eyes and smiles and lips and then deliver another. Was he?

She turned to face him. His features gave nothing away.

That should have made her angry, but it didn't. Instead, the fire she'd been ready to unleash on him flickered out. This was the façade, wasn't it? The face he showed when he wanted to pretend to the world that nothing got to him. The face he was showing to her to let her know the same. If there was a lie Max Martin told, this was it. The only one.

She searched his face, desperately looking for some hint she was right. His expression remained blank, but his jaw tightened. She started walking again, until they reached the little wooden door that led to the palazzo's tiny courtyard. Once there, she pushed the gate open and walked inside. She waited while he closed it behind him.

Nothing about this evening made sense, except the one truth she kept coming back to. Max Martin did the right thing, even if it killed him, even if it cost all that he had. So what about sending her away was 'right', and how on earth did she go about changing his mind?

Something drastic. Something shocking. Something he couldn't ignore. She was usually good at that. She dug down inside herself, poking in the dark corners of her imagination, to see if she could find anything to help, and came away empty, save for one thing—the only thing she'd been able to think about for the last few days.

'I love you,' she blurted out, and waited for his reaction.

He seemed to grow another layer of cement. 'I know.'

'Is that why you're sending me away?' she asked, a small wobble in her voice betraying her.

He nodded.

No breaking ranks and pulling her into his arms as he had done countless times since that evening on the lagoon. No echoed protestations of love. The silence grew around them. Here in the tiny courtyard with its high wall, it was complete.

So I tried to make him angry...

Fina's words floated through her head. It wasn't a great plan, but telling him she loved him had been a worse one. If at least she could get him to show *some* emotion, those walls might start to crack; she might be able to tell if he really felt anything for her at all, or whether it had just been another mirage this city had thrown up. Her heart was telling her one thing and her brain another and she had to stop the Ping-Pong match between them and just *know*.

It shouldn't be too hard. She seemed to have a special talent for lighting Max's fuse.

'You paint yourself as this big, strong man, who can rule the universe and isn't scared of anything, but underneath it you're nothing but a coward.'

He blinked. Very slowly.

Ruby felt the air pulse around her head. It had felt good to say those words. She hadn't anticipated how much.

'No wonder you can't get that design for the institute right, no wonder they had reservations about going with you. Because to create something stupendous, first you'd have to *feel*, to dream, but you don't have the courage.'

This time he didn't move at all. Now the air in the whole courtyard throbbed.

She was running out of things to say, things she thought might wound him, provoke some kind of a reaction. He might seem to be made of stone, but her blood was rushing round her veins, her cheeks heating. Feigned anger was quickly becoming the real deal.

He had to feel something for her—he had to. She drew in a deep breath, then gave it her best shot. 'Your father dug his own grave, you know. He finally imploded with the effort of keeping himself under lock and key, and you're going to end up the same way. He didn't deserve your mother, who's more patient and loving and forgiving than you will ever realise, and you're going to turn out just the same if you're not careful.'

She was on a roll now, couldn't stop herself if she wanted to. Hot tears began to stream down her face and her throat grew tight, making her voice scratchy. 'And you know what? Maybe it is better if I go, if I get as far away from you as I can, because I don't think I could stand being with a man like you anyway. I need someone who actually knows how to live and breathe, who knows how to love and be loved. Who, when he feels something for a woman, comes out and says so—

not just stands there like a lump of stone doing nothing!'

And he was like stone. Still.

She had no volume left now, only a hoarse whisper that only just made it past her lips. She started walking backwards towards the door. 'Well, you've got your wish. I'm leaving. And not because you're telling me to, but because I want to. I know you feel something for me!' She thumped her chest with her closed fist. 'I know it! But you can't—or won't—bring yourself to show it. And that means you don't deserve me, Max Martin, and you never will.'

Max stood in the courtyard long after Ruby had left him. It had taken all his effort to take what she'd thrown at him, every last ounce of his strength, and he had none left to open the door and follow. He'd wanted to kiss her fiercely, deeply, as if his very life depended on it—which it well might—and tell her just how much he cared, but he couldn't. Wouldn't.

He wondered if he was actually dripping blood, because that was what it felt like. Her words had stabbed him in the heart. This was what he'd always tried to avoid, what he'd always protected himself against. Did she think he didn't know that he didn't deserve her, that *he* wasn't what *she* needed? That was why he hadn't answered her question, had just let her assume the worst. He was letting her go, setting her free.

It felt as if he hadn't taken a breath in minutes, and he dragged one in now, the cool night air burning his lungs. He could see the lights on in the *piano nobile* of Ca' Damiani, could imagine her shoving clothes into her scruffy little ruck-sack, calling him every name under the sun.

A foolish part of him hoped that this wasn't it. That one day they'd meet again, and it would be the right time, that they'd both be ready, but he knew it was probably impossible. He didn't think she'd ever forgive him. And she had every rea-son not to.

But he'd had to do it this way. Otherwise she wouldn't have left, she'd have just kept trying, killing herself off piece by piece in the process. Damn her resilience.

He closed his eyes and swore out loud. In Ital-ian. And then he walked through the ground floor of the palazzo, the space that used to be the merchants' warehouse when the Damiani family had been part of the city's elite, and out of the boat door.

He needed to get out of this place, out of this glittering city that promised with one hand then took away with another.

He knew of somewhere much more appropriate. There were a number of deserted islands scattered across the lagoon that had once been quarantine islands, places where those with the plague had been imprisoned to stop them infecting the city, places where forgotten souls were still supposed to howl on a moonless night like this.

As the mist descended across the lagoon he started up the launch and headed away from the deceptive lights of the city, fully intending to join the dead in their howling.

Ruby flung all her belongings in her rucksack, but it took her considerably longer than three minutes. More like twenty. Maybe because she had to keep stopping to either wipe her eyes so she could see what she was doing or shout at the painting of the old man in a large black hat on the wall about what a pig-headed idiot his descendant was being.

When she was finally finished she crept next door to Sofia's room and watched the little girl sleeping, legs and arms flung carelessly over the covers. She pressed the gentlest of kisses to her temple, then quickly left, before she dripped tears on her and woke her up.

She met Fina in the hallway. 'You're back early!' she said, smiling, and then she stopped smiling. 'What has that fool of a son of mine done now?'

Ruby shrugged. 'He fired me.'

Fina went pale. *'What?'*

'Maybe "fired" is a little dramatic.' She sighed. 'It's the end of my contract. I knew it was only going to be a couple of weeks, but—' The tears clogging her throat prevented her from saying more.

Fina just walked forward and drew her into a hug. The kind of hug Ruby's mother used to give her when she was small and she hadn't realised she'd missed quite so badly. Ruby's torso shuddered and she clung on to Fina for a few long minutes before pulling away, putting the pieces of herself back together.

'You must come again,' Fina said, her eyes shining and her voice husky.

Ruby looked at her helplessly. She didn't know if she could return to this place. Somehow it had burrowed under her skin and she feared she'd always be reminded of what she'd almost had, of what it had snatched away from her on a fickle whim.

Fina must have understood that look, because she smiled softly. 'Well, when I come to London, then… You must take me out for tea and scones.'

A watery giggle escaped Ruby's lips. 'It's a deal.' She could just imagine Fina at the Ritz tea room, holding court and charming all the waiters, while the pianist played and the china clinked.

She checked her watch. 'I've ordered a taxi, so I really should go and get my things.'

'So soon?' Fina asked, looking a little forlorn.

Ruby nodded, and then Fina did, too. She was a woman who understood that when the time came a swift exit was the cleanest, if not the least painful, method of departure. Ruby was grateful for that.

She went and fetched her rucksack, hugged Fina once more, then descended the stone staircase for the last time and pushed the boat door open to walk onto the dock. The water taxi arrived only a few minutes later and Ruby climbed inside and looked steadfastly at the buildings on the other side of the canal as it turned around and pulled away.

She kept staring like that, stiff and unseeing, all the way to the train station. She didn't want to see any more of Venice. Not the details, anyway. Not the shapes of the arches or the patterns in the lace-like gothic façades. She was happier if it all just blurred into one big pool of light before her eyes.

CHAPTER SIXTEEN

'NO, I'M AFRAID the four o'clock flight won't do. The crew need to catch another connection out of Paris to Antananarivo at five. We need them on the two forty-five.'

The travel agent on the other end of Ruby's phone huffed.

She lowered her voice, made it softer. 'Mr Lange would be ever so grateful if you could swing it. I'd even arrange to have a box set of his last series sent round as a thank-you.'

She could tell he'd just opened his mouth to give her an excuse, but he paused. 'My mum really does love his programmes. Have you got the one with the penguins in it?'

'The Ice World of Antarctica?' Ruby asked, drawing a little black-and-white penguin with a bobble hat on in the corner of her office pad. Now, they'd make a great subject for a series of drawings. What was not to like? They were cute and walked funny.

'That's the one,' the man said, then chortled most unappealingly. 'And I'd have one less Christmas present to buy come December.'

Ruby pulled a face at the phone. Cheapskate. 'So can you help me?' she asked, almost purring down the line.

'Leave it with me,' he said, sounding a bit chirpier than when she'd first started talking to him. 'What did you say your name was again?'

'Ruby,' she said with a sigh in her voice. 'Ruby Lange.'

'Wow! You related?'

She resisted the urge to say *I'm his grandmother.*

'Yep. He's my dad.'

Ruby wilted a little further towards her desk. Just about every conversation she had these days ended up like this one. And she made hundreds of calls a week.

'It must be really cool to be Patrick Lange's daughter!' he said. 'What's it like working for him?'

Okay, *now* he wanted to be friendly and chatty, after making the last twenty minutes trying to get the flights for the next filming trip booked like squeezing blood from a stone.

'It's a blast,' she said as she drew a jagged crevice that her cartoon penguin was about to fall into. Still, she said her thank-yous and goodbyes politely and sweetly. No point zinging him until after the flights were booked.

The phone on her desk rang. She picked it up, half expecting it to be the travel guy again, and prepared herself to tell him, yes, she could send an autographed photograph to go with the DVDs, he just needed to let her know who her dad should make it out to, but it turned out to be Lucinda, her father's secretary.

'Mr Lange would like to see you in his office,' she said, then hung up.

Ruby stuck her tongue out at the phone. Lucinda always called Dad 'Mr Lange' in her presence; it was most weird. She was laced up as tight as the man in question was, so no wonder they'd been working well together for the last ten years.

Ruby shoved her chair away from her desk and picked up her pad and pencil. She ripped off the top sheet and hid it in her letter tray. Dad didn't really 'get' the doodling. Drawing while she was on the phone always helped her think, but if he saw it he'd only think she'd been slacking off, which she so hadn't.

She walked through the open-plan office and knocked on her father's door.

'Come!' he shouted.

Ruby obeyed.

'You wanted to see me?' she asked, choosing not to sit down. She had rather a lot to do today, what with the trip coming up. One of the crew wasn't British and needed an extra visa, and the paperwork was a nightmare.

Her father looked up from his desk. He was approaching sixty, but he was still fit and healthy, if a little weathered round the edges from all his travelling. 'Have you managed to source that special lens Cameron was after?' he asked.

She nodded. Their top cameraman had a brochure sitting on his desk and an appointment at one of the best video equipment suppliers to test it out in a few days' time.

'And how are we on getting that actress to do some of the voiceovers?'

Ruby hid a smile. 'That actress' was a multi-Oscar winner, who'd gone all fangirly when Ruby had called her people and asked if she'd like to work on the next series of Patrick Lange documentaries. 'Her office has just confirmed, but she won't be available for recording during September and October because she's shooting in Bulgaria.'

'Great.' Her father steepled his fingers and looked at her. 'And what about the tea?'

'In the kitchen,' she answered. Seriously, you'd have thought that finding a tin of his fresh leaf lapsang souchong when it had run out had been a national emergency. Thankfully, there was a little tea shop round the corner in Wardour Street that stocked just what she'd wanted.

'Do you want a cup?'

'Yes,' he said, and Ruby turned to go. 'But in a minute.'

She turned back again.

'Why don't you sit down?'

Uh-oh. He wasn't going to fire her, was he? She thought she'd been doing okay for the two months she'd been working here, and that incident with the delivery guy and the ten-thousand-pound camera really hadn't been her fault.

She sidled round the chair sitting opposite his desk and slid into it.

'I think we need to talk about your future here, Ruby.'

Oh, Lord. Here it came.

'Lucinda has let me know that she's going to have

to take maternity leave in the autumn, and I wondered if you'd be interested in filling in for her.'

Ruby's mouth dropped open. Whether it was because her father was offering her what was, in fact, a temporary promotion, or the idea of someone actually knocking frosty old Lucinda up, she didn't know.

'You've made quite an impression since you've been here,' he continued. 'I think it could be a nice step up for you.'

Ruby closed her eyes and opened them again. She'd obviously been transported into a parallel universe. 'I beg your pardon?'

Her father smiled at her, actually smiled! 'You've been doing a great job. Everyone thinks so.'

Ruby couldn't help the next words that fell out of her mouth. They just popped out before she had a chance to edit herself. 'Do *you*?'

He gave her a bemused smile, as if what she was asking was confusing or funny in some way. 'Of course I do. I always knew you could be good at something if you just settled to it.'

Yes, she was definitely in a parallel universe. It must have happened when she'd crossed the threshold into his office, because before then everyone and everything had been behaving as normal.

She looked back at him, searching his face. Was he really being serious?

What she saw shocked her.

Well, at least her time with Max had given her something more than bittersweet memories of a city she could probably never bear to visit again, because, just as she'd been able to look at Max, see the shell, know of its existence, but still catch glimpses of what was underneath, suddenly she could do the same with her father.

What she saw was different, of course. A little bit of paternal pride, more than a smidge of affection. Why had she never seen this before?

To be honest, she didn't know and she didn't care.

'What do you think?' her father said.

'I don't know,' she said truthfully. 'I've enjoyed the challenge of working here, and I'm not about to quit any time soon, but I'm just not sure it's…'

'You're not sure it's for you,' he finished for her softly.

She shook her head, afraid words would make the 'glimpses' disappear.

'Neither am I,' he said, standing up. 'But I thought I should offer you the opportunity.'

Ruby stood up, too. On a burst of emotion she ran over to her father and flung her arms around his neck. 'Thanks, Dad.'

He hugged her back, but muttered something about not making a fuss and nonsense at work.

Ruby pulled back and grinned at him. 'Sorry, I forgot. Lucinda would flay me alive if she heard me talking that way. I meant to say, "Thanks, Mr Lange".'

Real humour sparkled in his eyes, but he shooed her away. 'Go and get me that tea,' he said. 'And then it's probably about time you took your lunch break.'

Ruby looked at the clock. It was quarter to three already. No wonder her stomach was gurgling. She'd just been so busy that she'd forgotten to even think about lunch.

Ten minutes later she emerged from the Soho offices of One Planet Productions and turned left, her large slouchy patchwork bag tucked under her arm. She hadn't used it since that day she'd tried to blag a job in Thalia Benson's office, and she'd made herself bring it out today. One couldn't spend all one's life hiding from half the contents of one's wardrobe because of the memories they conjured up. Sometimes one had to suck it up and keep moving. Onwards and upwards. Her motto was still keeping her strong.

First stop was her favourite coffee shop for a latte and a wrap, and then she headed for the little park on Golden Square. She sat on her favourite bench on the south-west corner, under a tree, and ate her lunch. Once that was disposed of, she opened her bag and pulled out a large A4 sketchpad. She flipped the cover open and turned to the first blank page and began to draw.

Not a cheeky crab. She'd given up on those. Instead a grumpy pigeon.

Her whole sketchbook was filled with Grumpy Pigeon drawings. Pigeon on Nelson's Column, Pigeon at the palace with the Queen, Pigeon on the Tube…

Max had been right. This was her passion. She drew when she got up in the mornings now. She drew during her lunch break and she drew when she got home from work. Her flatmate was threatening to use the accumulated stack of papers in their flat to wallpaper the toilet.

Drawing also had another benefit. While she was throwing herself into it, she didn't think of Max.

Well, okay, she did, but the memories got pushed to the back instead of jostling themselves to the front, where they were sharp and painful.

She hadn't heard anything from him since her return to London or, presumably, at some point, his. At first she'd hoped it had all been some Venice-induced hysteria, that everything would right itself and he'd come and see her, make contact somehow. She should have remembered that Max wasn't big on communication.

But she had other things to concentrate on now. She was finally laying the path for her own future, rather than wandering around in the dark. Not only did she know her next step, she knew where she wanted to be in six months' time, and five years' time.

She had a big picture.

How sad there was a dark hole in it that should have been filled by someone, but he'd decided it wasn't his perfect fit.

She sighed and carried on drawing. She had a meeting with a young, funky greetings-card firm that had offices in Shoreditch. They loved the grumpy little pigeon and she was talking to them about trialling a series of cards. And the owner of the vintage fashion shop she'd worked at wanted her to do some drawings for their new publicity drive—too fabulous to be true fifties divas in sunglasses and headscarves. Then there was a friend of a friend who said he might be able to put her in touch with people who did book jackets. All in all, things were looking promising.

Oh, she knew she'd have to keep working at One Planet for at least another year or two, maybe more. But she enjoyed it and it was a way to pay the bills. That was what grown-ups did, didn't they? They dug in and worked hard for what they wanted instead of drifting around and waiting for the universe to drop it into their laps.

When her hour was up, she packed her stuff away and headed back to the office. When she walked up to her desk, Jax, one of the other production assistants, leaned over the partition between their desks.

'You had a telephone call while you were out,' he said.

'Oh?' Her heart did a little flip. *Stop it*, she told it. *You can't keep doing this every time the darn thing rings. It's pointless... Hopeless... Give it up, already.*

'Yeah. It was some guy from a travel company.'

Ruby sank into her chair and laid her head on her desk.

'He wants to know if you can get a set of DVDs for his nan, too.'

Serafina Martin glided into the high-rise offices of Martin & Martin, her sunglasses on and a scarf tied round her neck. Her son resisted the urge to roll his eyes as he watched her from the confines of his glass office. She wafted through the main floor in his direction, bestowing regal smiles on his employees.

He'd finally gone to his mother at the end of his stay in Venice, had given her the space and time to tell her side of the story. It hadn't been easy to hear it, but he'd done it. And upon his return to London he'd remembered what she'd said about never having seen his flat, so he'd invited her over.

Not that she'd consented to actually stay with him, but she'd very kindly let him foot the bill for a room at the Dorchester. It was probably worth it, anyway. If they were under each other's feet twenty-four-seven, they'd probably drive each other crazy and undo all the progress that they'd made.

They'd had a long heart-to-heart the night before

over dinner. He'd been aware that he'd listened to her side of the story in Venice, but he'd finally managed to release the things he'd needed to say, too. Like how he was sorry that he'd pushed her away for most of his life. He should have been loyal to both parents, not barricaded the doors against her as if she were the enemy. And he'd done it without Ruby there to egg him on, prod him when he was being stubborn. She would have been proud of him.

He ignored the stab of pain in his chest at the thought of her. That particular wound still hadn't closed, still dripped and weeped every day.

Neither he nor his mother were exactly sure what was going to happen from here on, but at least they were willing to try. He'd attempted to explain it to her. In actual words. The best he'd been able to do was tell her he wasn't sure how to deconstruct a relationship back to where it had been almost twenty years ago and start again, build it up in a different shape, with a different foundation.

Yes, he'd used a lot of building metaphors. He couldn't help it. He was new at this talking stuff, and it was the only way the words would come.

Fina had just leaned across the table and patted

his hand. 'You're the best architect I know, Massimo. You'll work it out.'

His mother finally reached his office door and entered without knocking, then collapsed gracefully into a leather chair and smiled. 'Shopping is so tiring, don't you think?'

Max frowned. If it was that tiring, you'd think she'd do less of it.

'I thought you said you'd be back at two. It's past four.'

She waved a hand, as if minutes and seconds were of no consequence. 'I was otherwise engaged.'

'Oh, yes?'

She fidgeted with her handbag. 'I met Ruby for afternoon tea at the Ritz.'

It was a warm August day outside, and the sun was glinting off the skyscrapers in the City of London, but Max's skin chilled and his heart lumbered to a stop.

'She showed me this,' she said, and handed him a small rectangular card in a cellophane sleeve. He turned it over to discover it was a greetings card. He hadn't seen the design before—a rather fierce-looking pigeon, who was standing guard at the Tower of London—but he recognised the style instantly.

She'd done it? She'd really done it?

His mother took the card back from him and tucked it in her handbag. 'I told her I thought the pigeon reminded me of someone we both knew, but she said she couldn't see it.'

'I do *not* scowl like that.'

'Darling,' she said sweetly, 'you're doing it now.'

He shook his head and walked back round the other side of his desk. 'How was she?' he asked, keeping his tone light, neutral, and messing with some bits of paper on his desk.

It had been hard knowing he was in the same city as her. He'd have considered moving back to Venice if the institute commission hadn't been ploughing ahead at full steam. They'd loved his new designs. Had eaten them up, and Vince McDermot had scurried off with his tail between his legs.

And it was all because of Ruby. He wished he could see her to tell her that.

Hell, he wished he could see her full stop. He looked up, realising his mother hadn't answered him.

'Honestly, Massimo,' she said, giving him that

same look she'd used to give him as a boy when he'd been caught stealing the family launch to go racing with his friends. 'When are you going to give up and admit you're head over heels for that girl?'

He stared back at her. Admitting it wasn't the problem. Forgetting it was.

And now he'd seen her drawings he knew he'd done the right thing. He'd only have weighed her down, held her back.

'Sometimes it's better to walk away. I thought you'd understand that better than anyone.'

His mother threw her hands in the air, indicating she did not know what to do with him. 'For a very intelligent man, my darling son, you can be incredibly stupid.'

'Thanks, Mamma,' he said between gritted teeth.

She stood up and walked over to him, her eyes warm and full of compassion. 'You are not your father, Massimo.'

He opened his mouth, but she held up her hand.

'Yes, you are very like him, but you are not a carbon copy.' She gave him a heartfelt look. 'You have a chance, darling, to make this right, to be happy. You can be what your father could not. I know it.'

It was surprising to discover just how much her faith warmed him. 'How can you be so sure?'

'Because I gave birth to you, because I know you. Because I've seen the way you've changed this summer.'

'I don't know how to tell her.'

She kissed him on the cheek and patted his arm. 'Skills like that are just like muscles. The more you use them, the stronger they get, and you've already made a start.'

Max thought of all the things he'd said to Ruby that last night in Venice. The way he'd seen her crumble in front of him. He wasn't sure words would ever be enough to repair that damage.

'Anyway,' she said, regaining some of her usual breezy air and heading for the door, 'I've got a taxi waiting downstairs and I need someone to carry my bags.'

Max raced after her. A taxi? They'd been talking for at least five minutes!

'What bags?' he said, sounding more like his usual self.

'Oh, I paid a little visit to Harrods before the Ritz.'

Four large bags were waiting for him in the back of the cab. He climbed in and passed them to his mother. The cabby smiled. He'd seemed quite happy to wait, with the meter ticking over at the speed of light. When the last one had hit the pavement, his mother gave him a gentle shove so he lost his balance and landed on the back seat.

'Go! Go and see Ruby.'

He looked back at her helplessly. He'd had no time to prepare, no time to think up any building-related images to help him explain. 'What will I say?'

'Just start, Massimo,' she said as she shut the door. 'The rest will come.'

And then she thumped the taxi on the roof and it sped off into the London traffic.

Ruby was supposed to be working, but she'd drifted off, staring out of the window. It wasn't something she usually did, but she'd looked up at the sky between the narrow buildings. It was exactly the same colour as the day they'd taken the speedboat out into the lagoon and found the secret beach, and for some reason she'd just ground to a halt.

She supposed she could call it a coffee break,

but she usually filled her breaks with sketching, because when they were filled with sketching it blocked out other things she didn't want to think about.

A large, heavy sigh deflated her ribcage.

She hadn't let herself look back much, but some of the memories were so lovely, even if it hurt like hell to think about them.

If only whistles were really magic…

Then she could put her lips together and let out that breathy little sound and everything she wanted would just rise from the London street to meet her.

She pursed her lips, and the noise that came out was both pathetic and forlorn.

Nothing happened. But why would it? This was London, not *La Serenissima*.

She shook herself. This was no way to live. *Come on, Ruby. Find yourself something to do, something to keep yourself occupied.* In this madhouse, it shouldn't be hard enough.

And, right on cue, a commotion erupted near the foyer. It was probably that clumsy motorbike delivery guy again. Thank goodness she was nowhere nearby to get blamed for his mishaps again.

The noise got louder. It was coming closer.

The One Planet office was large, but full of clutter and equipment, and the desks were separated by low screens to make cubicles. Ruby half stood and peered round the edge of hers to see what was going on.

There was a man walking down the central aisle, looking terribly grim, terribly stern. Everyone else cleared out of the way, but Ruby found she couldn't do anything but freeze as her pulse went crazy. If it got any faster, she was either going to have a stroke or shoot straight through the ceiling.

That was Max. Here in the office.

He spotted her—half crouching, half leaning out of her cubicle—and his trajectory changed.

Jax, who fancied himself a bit as the office bouncer, was on his heels. 'Hey, mate! Where d'you think you're going?'

'I'm going to see Ruby Lange,' Max replied, not taking his eyes off her.

Ruby stood up, and the folds of the skirt of her strawberry dress fell around her knees.

He stopped when he was about ten feet away. 'Wh-what do you want?' she stammered.

Faces appeared above partitions and some of

those who worked down the other end of the office drew closer to see what was going on.

Max just stared at her.

My, he looked amazing. All tall and gruff and… Max. She wanted to smile, to run to him, but she held back. Wasn't he going to say anything?

He stopped looking quite so stern. She saw him swallow.

He wasn't going to be able to do it, was he? He found saying what needed to be said impossible at the best of times. That was why she'd left him in Venice. Not because he hadn't cared, but because he'd been too much of a coward to show it. How was he going to do it with all these people looking on, all these strangers?

But then he straightened, grew even taller and smiled at her.

'I need you.'

The words hit her heart like an arrow, but this time she would not be wooed by them so easily. She needed to test them, to know their strength.

'I'm not a nanny any more,' she answered softly.

The heads of the onlookers swivelled back to look at Max.

The smile disappeared. 'I don't need a blasted nanny,' he told her. 'I need *you*, Ruby.'

'Why?' she almost whispered. Her heart thudded madly inside her chest, blood rushed in her ears. The seconds ticked by.

Details, Max. I need details.

He took a step forward. He was so close now that she could have reached out and touched him if she'd wanted to. The crowd shuffled closer. Someone walked in the door, back from a meeting and talking loudly on their mobile phone, and was shushed by at least five others.

'Because,' Max said, 'you are bright and beautiful and talented.'

She let out a shaky breath.

But he wasn't finished yet. 'Because you brought joy back into my dull, structured life.'

She felt a lump rise in her throat. She started to speak anyway, but he stopped her with a look.

'Because you challenge me, contradict me and generally drive me crazy.'

There was a rough laugh from behind her. 'Yes, but isn't she wonderful?'

Ruby turned to see her father standing at the end of the room. He was smiling. She looked back at Max, hardly knowing whether to laugh or cry.

'I wouldn't have it any other way.'

And then he was reaching for her, pulling her

to him and his lips were on hers and his arms crushed her to him.

'And because I love you,' he whispered in her ear, but she didn't mind that. These words were hers and hers alone. 'More than anything in this world, more than designing or building or even breathing. I promise you I am no longer ankle deep. I am in way, way, way over my head.'

She pulled back to look at him. 'Good answer,' she said, grinning. 'Because so am I.'

Max just laughed and kissed her again.

* * * * *

Mills & Boon® Large Print
October 2014

RAVELLI'S DEFIANT BRIDE
Lynne Graham

WHEN DA SILVA BREAKS THE RULES
Abby Green

THE HEARTBREAKER PRINCE
Kim Lawrence

THE MAN SHE CAN'T FORGET
Maggie Cox

A QUESTION OF HONOUR
Kate Walker

WHAT THE GREEK CAN'T RESIST
Maya Blake

AN HEIR TO BIND THEM
Dani Collins

BECOMING THE PRINCE'S WIFE
Rebecca Winters

NINE MONTHS TO CHANGE HIS LIFE
Marion Lennox

TAMING HER ITALIAN BOSS
Fiona Harper

SUMMER WITH THE MILLIONAIRE
Jessica Gilmore

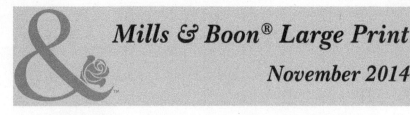

Mills & Boon® Large Print

November 2014